THE QUEUE

THE QUEUE

a novel

BASMA ABDEL AZIZ

TRANSLATED FROM THE ARABIC
BY ELISABETH JAQUETTE

 MELVILLE HOUSE
BROOKLYN · LONDON

THE QUEUE

First published by Dar Altanweer, Cairo
Copyright © 2013 by Basma Abdel Aziz
Translation copyright © 2016 by Elisabeth Jaquette

First Melville House printing: May 2016

Melville House Publishing   8 Blackstock Mews
        46 John Street   and   Islington
   Brooklyn, NY 11201   London N4 2BT

mhpbooks.com   facebook.com/mhpbooks   @melvillehouse

Library of Congress Cataloging-in-Publication Data
Names: Abd al-Aziz, Basmah, author. | Jaquette, Elisabeth, translator.
Title: The queue : a novel / Basma Abdel Aziz ; translated from the
   Arabic by Elisabeth Jaquette.
Other titles: الطابور. English
Description: Brooklyn : Melville House, 2016.
Identifiers: LCCN 2016009366 (print) | LCCN 2016015111 (ebook) |
   ISBN 9781612195162 (paperback) | ISBN 9781612195179 (ebook)
Subjects: LCSH: Egypt—Politics and government—21st century—
   Fiction. |Authoritarianism—Fiction. | BISAC: FICTION / Political.
   | FICTION / Literary. | GSAFD: Political fiction
Classification: LCC PJ7904.A95 T3313 2016 (print) | LCC PJ7904.A95
   (ebook) | DDC 892.7/37—dc23
LC record available at https://lccn.loc.gov/2016009366

Design by Marina Drukman

Printed in the United States of America
1   3   5   7   9   10   8   6   4   2

This book has been selected to receive financial assistance from
English PEN's PEN Translates programme, supported by Arts
Council England. English PEN exists to promote literature and
our understanding of it, to uphold writers' freedoms around the
world, to campaign against the persecution and imprisonment
of writers for stating their views, and to promote the friendly co-
operation of writers and the free exchange of ideas.

www.englishpen.org

ONE

Document No. 1

Patient Information:

Name:	*Yehya Gad el-Rab Saeed*
Age:	*38*
Marital Status:	*Single*
Place of Residence:	*District 9 – Building 1*
Occupation:	*Sales Representative*

The first thing Tarek did when he arrived that morning was ask the head nurse for the file. She brought him a transparent plastic folder that appeared to be sealed around the edges, with the words *Suspended Pending Approval by the Gate* written on the cover. He contemplated this weighty phrase, printed diagonally across a corner in bright red ink. The name *Yehya Gad el-Rab Saeed* was written on a rectangular white identification card affixed in the very center, and at the bottom of the card was a seven-digit number. The first half was probably part of the patient's national ID number, and the second half was a code referring to a type of file, something only the filing personnel really understood. Below the number came the name of the attending physician, his own name: *Dr. Tarek Fahmy.* Hundreds of times he had wished it would be struck from the label, but there was nothing to be done. It would remain there, a thorn in his side, until fate willed otherwise.

He walked into his office with the folder in hand, and Sabah, one of the nurses, followed behind him with a cup of coffee. She placed it on the edge of the antique wooden desk, just as she did every day, and then stood with her hands folded in front of her ample stomach. She began to yawn.

"Something else I can do for you, Dr. Tarek?"

"Stick around today, Sabah, I might need you for something." His tone was as calm and congenial as it always was, but to her he seemed unusually sullen.

"Of course, Doctor." She left and closed the door behind her.

Tarek was a serious, middle-aged man, one of the doctors

responsible for the hospital's emergency department. Sabah had known him for years, ever since he was a young trainee who spent nearly all his time with patients and barely ever went home. He didn't have many friends, didn't go out after work with his colleagues, and never skipped a shift like the others did. He was rather difficult to read; he kept to himself, shut himself up in his office during breaks, never chatted with the nurses in the hallway, and never mentioned a word about himself or his family. But everyone knew he was skilled at his job and—most important—that he had a good heart.

Tarek took a sip of coffee and began to pace back and forth across the room, his eyes on the folder. He finally settled back in his leather chair, opened one of the edges, and removed the file inside to review it again.

For him, actually handling a patient's file was a rare occasion. These documents usually contained only basic information, the kind taken from all patients, scribbled down quickly and often haphazardly. When the doctors and nurses tired of filling out forms, they just wrote down the person's name and age and that was it. But here, someone had thoroughly recorded all the patient's personal information; no space was left blank. Every question had an answer, even questions a doctor might not be concerned with. Even questions an average person might be surprised to see in a medical file.

Yehya Gad el-Rab Saeed, 38 years old, Single, Place of Residence: District 9 – Building 1, Occupation: Sales Representative... Tarek had gone over these basic details again and again until he knew them by heart, although they were not what interested him most about the patient.

He pushed the first document aside and took out the next one. There was a series of knocks on the door, and he quickly put everything back in the folder, closed it, and hid it in his desk drawer. He sat up straight as Sabah entered again, carrying a new file in her hand.

"There's a patient asking for you, Doctor. Should I tell him you're busy?"

He didn't feel like taking on any other work just now. As soon as he'd begun to review Yehya Gad el-Rab Saeed's file, he'd been transported to a place where he couldn't bear to be around other people. But he also didn't want to have to explain himself to Sabah, so he told her to take the patient to an examination room and wait for him there. He was considering whether he should return the folder to the filing room instead of leaving it there in his office when he remembered the keys sitting on his desk. He slipped on his white coat and left the room, softly closing the door behind him and making sure to turn the key twice in the lock before carefully placing it in his shirt pocket.

The examination only took a few minutes. He asked the patient a few quick questions, hastily examined him, and scribbled down a diagnosis and treatment, but his mind wandered back to the folder he'd left in his desk. He considered making a copy of the file and taking it home, where he could read and reflect upon it without interruption, but he pushed the idea aside, afraid of the consequences. He was beginning to understand that this was no longer a trivial matter; it was of interest outside the hospital administration's jurisdiction as well.

Tarek was a man who didn't overstep boundaries, a man who'd never been to the Gate, not once in his life. No questions, no problems—life passed him by both predictably and monotonously, just as he liked it. He'd finished his studies and received his master's degree, and it wouldn't be long now before he could open his own clinic. He'd even asked a colleague out on a date not long ago. The only thing hindering this stable, traditional plan of his was Yehya Gad el-Rab Saeed.

Why had he stayed in the hospital that day, when he always left right after finishing his shift? Why had he insisted on checking on the injured, resolutely doing all he could to treat their wounds and stitch them up before the ambulance took them away to the military hospital? Why had he been drawn to Yehya in particular, rushing to perform an X-ray and ignoring everyone else? His head was all muddled; the answers and details steadily slipped away. There were parts of that day that he did remember, and he had reviewed them over the course of the intervening weeks, but these were rapidly outnumbered by parts he couldn't recall. It was as if entire pieces of what had happened were simply gone. Looking back through the file should have helped, but instead it only exacerbated his sense of confusion.

On his way back to his office, he walked past the empty examination rooms and saw several new doctors drinking tea and coffee by the radio. He paused a minute to listen: it was the Youth Station presenter speaking on the air with a call-in guest. The presenter asked the guest about her children, who were still in school, and applauded their nationalist values, which were so worthy of emulation. How honorable they were not to leave the house when the Disgraceful Events broke out! What laudable principles they had, which had kept them from being swept up in lies or spreading false rumors themselves.

The guest was delighted by the praise lavished upon her—she spared no effort on her children, she added excitedly. She offered them constant guidance, so they would grow up knowing what was good for them, and she'd never feared they would stray from what was proper. Bewildered, Tarek shook his head. He made his way back toward the head nurse. He asked her if she would let him finish some important paperwork in his office without interruption, and she told him she would divide his patients among his colleagues. She summoned Sabah, who had finished her breakfast, and told her to distribute the files equally among the other rooms.

Tarek returned to his leather chair, the presenter's words still ringing in his ears. The country had been through tumultuous times in recent years, though he'd tried to keep his distance from it all. Just like everyone else, he'd heard about the Disgraceful Events when they occurred, or perhaps shortly after they began. But he hadn't been there, didn't know much about it, and had never been interested in finding out more. He'd heard passing comments from colleagues and acquaintances, neighbors, and fellow passengers on public transport, and had formed a vague image of the Events, hazy in the details but enough for him to participate when people brought it up in conversation. If asked, he would produce an opinion about how certain people—who were angry about being forced to follow the strict order the Gate had imposed soon after it appeared—had caused an unnecessary uproar. They'd rejected its new rules, and wanted to create a different, less authoritarian system, as Tarek had understood. They'd wanted a more lenient regime, one perhaps more tolerant, but, in Tarek's personal opinion, it was also less stable.

The Events had begun when a small group of people held a protest on a street leading to the square. There weren't many of them, but they boldly condemned the Gate's injustice and tyranny. Their demands were lofty, the stuff of dreams, another doctor told Tarek during one of their night shifts together:

the protestors called for the dissolution of the Gate and ev-erything it stood for. Before long, others joined the demon-strations, too. They chanted with passion, their numbers grew, and the protest started to move, but they were quickly confronted by the Gate's newly formed security units. These accused the protesters of overstepping their bounds, and said they wouldn't tolerate such insulting behavior. Then the forces attacked, to "return people to their senses," beating them bru-tally. When the injured protestors scattered in retreat and ran into the side streets, they were accused of "spreading chaos," and attempting to undermine the blessed security that had fi-nally—thankfully—returned under the Gate's rule.

The protesters quickly regrouped and met the security forces again, in a street battle that lasted for four days. More and more people fell. The Quell Force had been created to sup-press this kind of riot and was better armed than any govern-ment agency before it. On the final day, it cleared the square effortlessly, wiping out everyone at the rally in just a few hours. In the end, the Gate and its guardians had prevailed, and they emerged stronger than before.

Tarek had never questioned the Gate's definitive and crushing triumph. But he wasn't altogether enthusiastic about it, either, particularly given the sorts of injuries he'd attended to in the emergency room. He'd seen firsthand the how the Gate had secured its victory, and he knew that such opposition wasn't likely to build again.

The Gate had come into power many years earlier, in the wake of a popular uprising known as the First Storm. Tarek had never been one for history, but he remembered reading about these winds of change that had once swept the whole country. Ordinary people rose up, defeated the security forces on the streets, overcame the old guard's defenses, and nearly forced the ruler to surrender. But unfortunately—or perhaps it was fortunately?—things hadn't continued as they'd begun. The movement fractured before it was able to overthrow the regime. Some people used the gains they'd made to secure their own position and power. Others continued the fight against the regime, leaving a path of destruction in their wake. Some armed themselves in anticipation of a counterattack. Still others were wary because the ruler might manage to remain in power, and slipped away to make their own private deals with him.

Soon the situation unraveled, and different groups who had taken part in the First Storm accused one another of betrayal. They were so entrenched in their own conflicts that they forgot about the ruler, who started to rally his inner circle and regained influence on the ground. While the people were distracted with their squabbles, the old guard regrouped and began to rebuild. Not long after this, the Gate appeared.

Tarek stood up from his chair. He felt drained, even though he'd barely accomplished anything since arriving that day. He scanned a page from the file in front of him again, for this patient whose problems he didn't entirely remember, and then asked for permission to leave early, with an excuse about a cough he said had lingered for days.

THE QUEUE

In the fierce heat, Yehya stood in a long queue that extended from the end of the wide street all the way to the Gate. A whole hour and he'd moved no more than two steps forward, and that wasn't because there had been progress at the front of the queue. Some inexperienced soul—probably someone who had never been to the Gate before—was overcome with boredom, got discouraged, and left.

The sun was beating down on his left side, dividing him in two just as it did every day in the noon heat. His body felt heavy, but he didn't move from his place in the queue. In front of him stood a tall woman, her eyes darting around. She wore a flimsy black *galabeya* and a black veil, which hung alongside her bare neck, mingling with the wrinkles and creases it fell across. The young man standing behind him asked what time the Gate opened, and Yehya shrugged. He had no idea when it would finally happen. But he still left his house each morning, dragging his feet and his stomach and his pelvis, all of it heavy, to stand in the queue without ever reaching the Gate.

The woman was dark, just like her clothes; slender and elderly but naturally strong. Given her sturdy build and the milky whites of her eyes, Yehya guessed she was from the far south. She turned halfway around, quickly sizing him up with a sharp glance, and seeming to find him acceptable, she launched headlong into conversation.

She'd arrived at the Gate yesterday, she said; she came to file a complaint and get a certificate notarized while she was there. She fell silent for a moment, to give him the opportunity to ask her what the certificate was for, but Yehya said nothing. She started up again, despite his indifference, saying that for the first time in her life she hadn't been able to buy government-made *baladi* bread, the kind she'd bought for years without fail. She looked at him again, expecting to have aroused his curiosity, but he was preoccupied and hadn't followed what she was saying. Annoyed, she turned away and looked around again, then picked up her story where she'd left off, finding more attentive ears among her other neighbors.

The plump woman in front of her adjusted her turquoise veil with both hands and stepped closer—the subject of an official complaint had won her over. She had a young face, despite how heavy she was; she was maybe thirty years old, with thin eyebrows, a sharp nose, and well-cared-for skin. She sympathized with the old woman and asked in surprise whether bread, too, was really now that hard to come by. In a thick Southern accent, the old woman began her story.

"That low-down son of a bitch, that man, I was a customer of his for ten years, and every day I get my bread from him, so what happened, eh? I go just like I do every morning, to get my two pieces of *baladi* bread, and he asks me, 'Who did you pick?' I tell him I checked the box next to the candidate with the pyramid symbol. He gets real mad, flashes his teeth, and tells me, 'I know your kind, the whip is what people like you deserve. Lady, didn't I give you the purple list so you'd pick one of those candidates?' So I shut up and hold out a one-pound note, but he throws it on the ground, snatches back both pieces of bread, and shouts at me, 'We don't have any bread! And don't come back!' The nerve of that man! So I go to the European bakery, but it was all shut down. The next morning I go out early, to the bakeries in the market, but turns out they heard what happened, too. They tell me the same thing and won't let me have any bread, either. My neighbor told me if that's the way it is, I should file a complaint with the Gate. Told me I needed to apply for a certificate—I forget what it's called—the one with a government stamp, 'cause they'll be sure to ask me for one when my complaint gets investigated." She shoved her hand into her vast *galabeya* and pulled out a small piece of cardboard, the words *Certificate of True Citizenship* written upon it.

The young woman patted the old woman's shoulder consolingly. Things weren't what they used to be, she thought, and they weren't going to get better any time soon. Politics had eaten away at people's heads until they in turn had begun to devour one another. She too had chosen the pyramid symbol on her ballot, but unlike the old woman, she never admitted who she'd actually voted for, not to anyone. If she was honest with herself, she was too scared. In recent months the question "Who did you pick?" had spread like the plague, but she was cautious, wary, and knew it was better to keep quiet. Things had gotten to the point where she often relied on an old trick to avoid answering. Her response each time was to turn the question around on whoever was asking and follow their reply—whatever it was—with a wink, a shy smile, and the reliable phrase: "That's who I voted for, too."

She'd only made a mistake once, a few days ago. A student in the Arabic class she taught handed in an essay she'd written, just an ordinary homework assignment, the kind all students did. The girl had written a long, brilliant paper about the conditions in the district where she lived, and then went on to speak more broadly about the state of the country and developments in the region. The girl's words echoed what Ines herself might say if no one were listening. She was so impressed that she began to doubt the student, suspecting that one of the girl's older sisters, or perhaps a parent, had written the essay. The students usually did better on homework than exams, but perhaps someone else had written at least the outline for her. The girl swore she hadn't had help from anyone in her family, that every thought and sentence was hers alone. Ines was inclined to believe her, so she gave the student a nearly perfect grade, had the class applaud her, and asked the girl to read her essay in front of the other students, as an example of outstanding work.

The next day, the girl was absent from school. A soft-spoken inspector arrived at the principal's office, asking to see Ines's Personnel File and inquiring as to how she'd been hired. He informed the principal that Ines was missing certain forms and that she needed to go to the Gate to obtain a Certificate of True Citizenship. He told him that if she didn't, he would be forced to refer her to the Administrative Office, where she would be retested and reevaluated, and they would determine whether it was truly in everyone's best interest for her to continue as a teacher. Before leaving the school, he left a cassette tape with the principal. Ines later learned that it was a recording of the girl reading her assignment.

Unlike other children, who flit from one idea to the next, Ines had always wanted to be a teacher. As a child she often lined up her dolls in a long row on the bed, taking a ruler in hand and explaining a lesson. She would ask them questions, one doll after the next, and imagined their answers. When she grew a bit older, she continued her favorite game by seating the neighbors' children in a row on the stairs of their building. Holding a branch she'd snapped off a tree, she gave her students colored stones as rewards or smacked their shoulders with the stick to reprimand them for their ignorance. But now, she was the one standing there like a student who had committed the gravest mistake, waiting to be disciplined. Maybe this one slip-up would prevent her from pursuing the only thing she knew how to do. She glanced at the others standing in the queue before pausing to contemplate Yehya's gaunt face. He was staring off into the distance.

Yehya hadn't interrupted the old woman since she'd begun to talk. He was oblivious to her, immersed in his own thoughts. He didn't hear a word of her story, or of the other conversations around him, but she hadn't stopped chattering away, nor had she given up her stubborn efforts to win his attention, as if it were a personal challenge. Ines watched the scene unfold. "Everyone's got enough of their own problems," she whispered under her breath.

Weariness crept across Yehya's face, and deep furrows formed between his eyebrows. Nagy, who was squatting on the ground beside his friend, had become restless and wanted to leave. Yehya bent over slightly and groaned softly, and Nagy stood up and grabbed Yehya's arm, telling him to sit in his place for a little while. He'd been reclining under the shade of a yellow cloth banner whose colors had faded in the weeks since the election but still showed the candidate's face, his big red heart logo, and the familiar violet party symbol. Yehya turned down Nagy's offer, not out of pride, but because the pain was so bad he couldn't bend his knees to lower his body that short distance to the ground. He searched in his pocket for a strip of the painkillers he always carried with him but found just an empty packet. A handsome young man in front of them had been eavesdropping over Nagy's shoulder, and he offered a couple of pills of an over-the-counter medicine, the kind for headaches. He also offered to save Yehya's place in the queue, if he wanted to lie down at the man's place for a bit, but Nagy thanked him on Yehya's behalf, saying he'd heard that the Gate would open today. It seemed certain this time, he said, and they couldn't miss a chance that might not come again soon.

The young man took a step closer and, whispering, asked them what they needed from the Gate. Yehya gave Nagy a soft jab in the side, so slight that no one else noticed, and quickly replied, "Oh nothing, just permission for medical treatment. I've got this silly little stomach pain. It keeps me up at night, and I need some special medicine for it—the doctor gave me a prescription when I went to the hospital, and I asked around at several pharmacies, but no one's got it. People who take it say it's available in public clinics, but you know how it is— they need permission from the Gate to fill your prescription."

The young man nodded solemnly and looked like he was about to say something else, but then changed his mind and returned to where he'd been standing. The old woman interjected, saying that medicine only made you sicker, while a cup of warm mint tea would bring back his health and get rid of his pain too. She tutted disapprovingly, leaned over to Ines, and pushed some dried mint stalks into her hand. "Tomorrow I'll get some hot water from the coffee shop around the corner and make you tea with this," she said. Nagy leaned over and whispered in Yehya's ear that if he had half the faith she did, it would do him a lot of good. With a grin, Yehya shot back, "If you had half her faith, we wouldn't have to listen to you ramble on all the time."

UM MABROUK

Um Mabrouk had just finished tidying up the last room when it was time for her to leave. She went into the bathroom, shut the door behind her, and changed out of her wet clothes, washed her face, and put on a clean *galabeya* and low heels. She made sure she had everything in her handbag, felt around for the envelope inside it for the third time, and then said goodbye to the employees who were still in the office and rushed off, just managing to squeeze herself into a microbus before it pulled away from the sidewalk. When she arrived at the Gate there was a river of people flooding the street, and as she got off at the corner, she snagged her stocking on a bit of metal jutting out from the bottom of the microbus door that never closed. She hitched up the hem of her *galabeya* and saw a wide hole quickly unraveling upward. Her last bottle of nail polish had just run out, but she kept smiling all the same. She walked alongside the queue, assuring people she wasn't skipping ahead of them but had just come searching for a relative, and passed dozens of people before she arrived at Yehya. She recognized him by the back of his head before seeing his face, and reached out to shake his hand.

"Hello, Yehya. I've got a letter for you from the office."

Yehya seemed concerned by her sudden arrival, but he tried to appear welcoming, as if he'd been expecting her.

"*Ahlan, ahlan* . . . how're you doing, Um Mabrouk? I'm so

glad you managed to make it." She handed him the envelope, a smile still on her lips.

"I don't know what's inside—good news, I hope. Anything else I can do for you?"

"Thanks, you really shouldn't have gone to all this trouble."

Um Mabrouk rushed off, and Yehya's heart trembled, sending convulsions down his left side and bringing him a new wave of pain. A faint shudder shook his hand as he held the envelope, which Nagy urged him to open. The only thing inside was an unlined white page with a few handwritten sentences.

> *Dear Yehya, I hope you're doing well. I wanted to tell you that a doctor came to the office yesterday looking for you, he was wearing a military uniform and said he works at Zephyr Hospital, but he didn't ask about anything else. Let's meet soon. Amani.*

After reading the letter, Yehya fell into deep and troubled thought. He didn't want anything to do with the hospital or anyone in it. He hadn't seen Amani for a whole week; they'd agreed on a time to meet and talk about what was happening, but he was stuck here in the queue. He passed most of the day there and sometimes even spent the night, as many others did. Nagy had offered to bring him a tent to sleep in, but he'd turned it down. He would rather be like everyone else, chatting until the early hours of the morning and then nodding off for an hour or two in his place. People around him stood there so resolutely, he hadn't seen many sleeping or even sitting down in recent days. Everyone expected the queue to move at any minute, and they wanted to be ready. He found himself doing the same, even though he didn't believe what they told him about the Gate—that it might open at dawn, or even deep in the middle of the night.

On her way back home, Um Mabrouk sank into a seat on the old metro, enjoying a moment of rest after a long, tiring day. In her heart, she knew she couldn't work this hard anymore, not like she had when she was young and in full health. Um Mabrouk had first worked for Amani's mother. Then Amani had introduced her to the owner of the company she worked for, and he'd hired her to clean, work in the kitchen, and lend a hand around the office three days a week. When Amani's mother passed away, followed soon after by her father, Um Mabrouk started to work at Amani's office full-time: five days a week, morning to afternoon, with only a few minutes for a lunch break. When the expenses for her apartment and children rose like floodwaters and she could barely stay afloat, she took on two more small houses for her days off. Um Mabrouk's face was lined with sorrow. If fate hadn't been so hard on her, she wouldn't have been tossed from cleaning one house to another, working so many jobs.

Her train of thought was broken by a large, dirty-looking man who got into the metro car as the woman across from her rose from her seat. He rushed over in his tattered rags, rubbing up against Um Mabrouk's knees as he slumped into the vacant seat. He stuck his head out the window and suddenly began singing gruffly and sucking at his long dusty hair. Um Mabrouk silently promised herself that despite how bad he smelled she wouldn't get up until her stop; she could so rarely relax, and he was the least of her troubles. She watched him cautiously and edged her legs away, but that didn't stop the man, who seemed half-crazed, from curiously reaching out to grab at her breasts. Um Mabrouk jumped up, screaming and cursing at him, and hit him with her bag, which opened up, and the broken old rotary phone she'd taken from the office to repair fell onto the floor. The man panicked at the clatter, leapt toward the metro door in fright, and jumped out before the train stopped at the next station.

Shouts of fear and confusion rose up from the women around her. She heard mutters of shame from a few passengers, and a tall man whispered that a woman's place was in the house, his gaze fixed on the ground. Someone else quoted a passage from the Greater Book, and although she couldn't make out what he said, she sensed from his tone that it was directed at her. A young boy came up to her and asked if she was hurt; he was no more than twelve and wearing a school uniform that was clearly old but well kept. "Bless you, darling," she said, as she patted him on his shaved head. She continued the string of insults she'd begun, and then bent over to pick up the telephone and reattach the handset, and sat down again. The man had really scared her, but she blamed herself. After all, she'd decided not to give up her seat across from him, and she had sat there while the rest of the passengers had given him space as soon as they'd seen him.

She was forever cursed with bad luck, and there was no end to her problems, no matter how much she tried to set things right. Her eight-year-old son was sick with a bad kidney and was always in and out of the hospital for more treatments. She'd taken him in several times in just the past month, and watched as his slender body was pumped with what seemed like gallons of medicine. Her two older daughters couldn't help with the bills because they were both weak with rheumatic heart disease. By the time the doctor had read her the results of the X-rays and medical tests that had diagnosed their condition, they had already fallen far behind in school.

All she had was two rooms in a damp ramshackle apartment, buried deep in an alleyway in the old District 3 where the sewers bubbled over, and a husband who never left the coffee shop, who'd quit his job and wandered around idly in search of hash and pills. She saw him only when he ran out of the money he took from her small salary, sometimes by pleading with her and sometimes by force. Every so often at night he would leave the coffee shop and come begging, demanding more money, and when she scolded him he berated her and sometimes even beat her. On top of all that, two months ago she'd fallen and broken her hand while cleaning the ceiling in the office, and then she broke her left foot when she'd jumped off a microbus. The pain hadn't let up since then. As if everything else wasn't enough.

Neighbors who noticed her never-ending woes advised her to find out why she suffered such misfortune, and so she did. She visited the High Sheikh, before that too was forbidden—forbidden, at least, without a permit from the Gate—and he told her bad luck followed her because she'd neglected her prayers. The remedy to poverty was to bow down and pray and to stop her grousing and complaining. Her head filled with so many words, and a way out of this suffering seemed to open up before her. Tears of humble remorse flowed down her cheeks, and she swore she would uphold her religious duties and never miss a prayer. She even bought a white scarf to keep at Amani's mother's house so she would be sure to have one for praying there, but she stuck to her new commitment for fewer than two weeks and her bad luck never left her. Some days she forgot, and on others she put off her ablution until she finished work. At the end of the day she would discover she had all her prayers left to do, and, exhausted, she'd vow to start anew the next day at dawn. But then she'd wake up late and run straight out the door, intending to make it up throughout the day, and on it would go. She had so much trouble sticking to what she set out to do, sometimes she wondered if she might even be possessed by an evil spirit.

She walked the rest of the way home from the metro station, and before she crossed the crumbling wooden threshold she took off her shoes and tucked them under her right arm. She climbed the stairs with feet as rough as the slanted steps, which were pocked with knots and holes. She pushed open the flimsy front door, dropped her shoes, and called for her son, Mabrouk. She took out the phone and gave it to him, smiling so wide for him that her eyes scrunched up into two tiny dots. But Mabrouk cried when he lifted the speaker to his ear and didn't hear the dial tone he remembered from when they'd once had a landline, back when he was a baby. Surrounded by a tangle of wires, she promised him that the dial tone would be there in just a few days. She remembered the notice she'd received from the Gate a year earlier, stating that she wasn't entitled to a phone line due to misconduct. But that must have been a mistake, she told Mabrouk now; she was sure the Gate would sort it out soon.

TWO

Document No. 2

Time, Location, and Circumstances of the Injury

The patient, Yehya Gad el-Rab Saeed, arrived at the reception desk at 2:45 p.m. on Tuesday, June 18. Those accompanying him stated he was injured at approximately 1:30 p.m. while passing through District 9, where the Events occurred. They stated that he left company headquarters to meet some clients and employees on the other side of the square when clashes between unknown persons began. The unrest escalated and spread to the surrounding streets. Several of them witnessed his attempt to leave the area. He was injured, however, and they were unable to identify his assailant. They carried him to the hospital on their shoulders, and he was conscious upon arrival, despite a significant loss of blood. They stated that his documents were lost en route, and the bag of merchandise he had been carrying was stolen. As such, there is no evidence of the veracity of their account.

Attached to this file is a detailed list of the names of those accompanying the patient.

Receptionist's Signature

Tarek mulled over the words jumbled together on the second document with irritation. Yehya's blood had drenched the floor and the bedsheets when he arrived at the hospital. If a doctor or nurse had been with him when he'd been injured, she would have made the others carry him more carefully. Doing so would have taken just enough time for them to arrive at the emergency room an hour or so after Tarek's shift had ended, and the name of another doctor would have been at the end of this file: perhaps Ahmed or Bahaa or even Samah. Or if they'd just waited for one of the ambulances from Zephyr Hospital to arrive at the square, that would have been it; Tarek wouldn't have run into them in the emergency room at all. But Yehya had come straight to him, the first of the arrivals, his body a map of the battle. Tarek removed the pencil he always kept in his coat pocket and began to doodle on the page, absorbed in the lines and curves he'd begun to create, summoning an artistic side he had long since abandoned, one detached from everything else surrounding him. A couple of minutes passed before he awoke from his reverie. He abandoned his rumination about the Events, tossed the pencil down, and stood up from his leather chair.

On half of the second document, in a space without words, he had drawn a figure resembling Yehya, nearly naked, and a small, solid circle, completely shaded in, occupying a space in the lower left part of his stomach. He opened the door, asked Sabah for another cup of black coffee, and then turned around, glancing over at his desk. He picked up an eraser and carefully erased what he'd drawn. He lifted the paper up to the light coming in through the window and looked at Yehya's outline and the shadow of the solid circle, no longer there.

THE WAY TO AMANI

About a week after Um Mabrouk arrived with the letter, two events took place that sparked curiosity and commotion in the queue. First, the elderly woman from the South, who hadn't sat down to rest for a moment since arriving, suddenly collapsed. Her son appeared instantly, a tan young man who carried her off before anyone could ask how he'd known she'd fainted. Some said she was overcome with fatigue and her spirit had risen to meet its Creator, while others said she had survived and was put in intensive care in the military hospital, where they could monitor how her heart and lungs were functioning. But the man in the *galabeya*, who had appeared in the queue quite suddenly without explanation, proclaimed this a sign that God was angry because she had wronged herself and all other citizens. Despite coming to the Gate and acknowledging what she had done, she did not repent or hide the error of her ways—instead she flaunted it, unabashedly parading it around. Even worse, instead of coming to submit an apology or ask God for forgiveness, she was bent on filing a complaint, as if she were the one who'd been wronged. Silence gathered around him, as he raised his palms to the sky and called out: "Only those who have gone astray picked pyramid candidates!"

The second event was the appearance of Ehab, who announced straightaway that he was a journalist. He didn't try to hide it, as reporters who'd arrived before him often had. He considered himself above reserving a place in the queue and instead began to work his way up and down past the people waiting, asking questions and recording everything in a little notebook. He'd started out as a rioter, an activist flush with enthusiasm, and the vast distances he traversed throughout the day still never seemed to tire him.

Meanwhile, the people standing at the threshold of the Gate estimated that there were three whole kilometers between them and the end of the queue—much to the chagrin of those near the end, who insisted they weren't nearly that far away. At the queue's midpoint, the two sides were about to erupt into a brawl over their varying estimations of the distance when a well-known surveyor standing in the middle of the queue intervened and volunteered to settle the matter. Asking for a bit of quiet, he ran some quick calculations, using his geographical knowledge of the area, information provided to him by both parties (representatives from the beginning and the end of the queue), and a detailed description of the area's various landmarks and general terrain. He made sure to include land now occupied by the queue's most recent additions, those who had joined throughout the night. Finally, with pen and paper in hand, the man announced that the distance was in fact approximately two kilometers. Those who had been at each other's throats just a moment before were satisfied and stopped shouting, and everyone returned to their places, pleased with the results.

Yehya felt that the day had already been plenty eventful, in contrast to the endless empty days that had come before it. People in the queue had enough to debate and discuss until nightfall, and Yehya thought it unlikely that yet another big event—like the opening of the Gate—would happen as well. Besides, the Gate wouldn't reopen without releasing some kind of announcement beforehand. He was becoming annoyed with Ehab and his questions, the outrage he could conjure out of thin air, his insistence on launching into ridiculous subjects and extracting answers to questions that were of no consequence to anyone else. His thoughts returned to Amani, and he realized he should hurry to visit her. It didn't look like anything else was going to happen at the Gate today. Although momentum seemed to be building, things happened slowly here, and leaving for a little while wouldn't do any harm.

As soon as the old Southern woman was taken away, Ines— that foolish young teacher he considered a bit strange—had appeared in front of him. Everyone had something to say to her, and she tirelessly listened to their trifling concerns and endless stories, but no one had ever heard her utter anything important or useful. Yehya wasn't at all inclined to speak to her. He didn't want to tell her he would be leaving for a couple of hours, despite the conventions of the queue, which had developed over the passing days and were now practically set in stone. If he told the people around him a bit about himself and where he was going, he would be allowed to keep his place in the queue—even if he left for a long time—but Yehya decided to shirk tradition and take the risk. He left without a word and calmly slipped away. Nagy caught up with him, instinctively falling into step without knowing where they were headed.

The weather was hot and humid, and as the sun climbed upward, it appeared to dissolve the sky behind it. In front of them, the street looked like it had just emerged from an invisible war: papers strewn everywhere, broken bottles scattered on the ground, boxes of garbage plucked out of the bins, piles of burning rubber tires still spouting smoke and occasionally flames. Nagy realized that it had been a while since he'd heard any news from Tarek. He asked Yehya, who waved the question away. He hadn't seen or called Tarek since that dismal night in his office, when the doctor had shown him those documents. They left the main road and headed toward Amani's building, Yehya instinctively taking the side streets. They passed several sleepy cafés and a few small shops lining the road, most closed for the day behind heavy metal grates, even though it was barely four o'clock in the afternoon.

Nagy said he'd heard many shops had closed for good. So many shopkeepers spent so long in the queue that they couldn't buy or sell anything or supervise their employees, and so they decided to get rid of their merchandise. He heard that even people who didn't need to join the queue did the same when the Disgraceful Events began; they closed their businesses one after another, fearing the losses that loomed on the horizon. A relative of his, a man in the know, told him that sometimes other people didn't believe that the shops were vacant and broke in. When they didn't find what they'd come for, they took everything they could carry: computers and chairs, cheese cutters and deli-meat slicers. Even metal padlocks disappeared off doors in those parts of town.

Yehya and Nagy wandered through the near-empty streets. No one knew when rush hour was anymore; there were no set working hours, no schedules or routines. Students left school at all sorts of times, daily rumors determined when employees headed home, and many people had chosen to abandon their work completely and camp out at the Gate, hoping they might be able to take care of their paperwork that had been delayed there. The new decrees and regulations spared no one.

Yehya shook his head in silence. Since the Gate had materialized and insinuated itself into everything, people didn't know where its affairs ended and their own began. The Gate had appeared rather suddenly as the First Storm died down, long before the Disgraceful Events occurred. The ruler at the time had been an unjust one, and popular resistance gathered to oppose him. The ensuing uprising wracked his reputation and jeopardized his properties and those of his cronies. It threatened to sweep away the system he and his inner circle found so agreeable and desperately wanted to preserve. One night, as tensions were building, the ruler broadcast a short speech on television, in which he spoke of "the necessity of reining in the situation." There was no other harbinger of the Gate's appearance: the next day, people awoke and it was simply there.

At first no one knew what this immense and awe-inspiring structure was that simply offered its name—the Main Gate of the Northern Building—as the pretext for its existence. Yet it was not long before people realized the importance that it now played in their lives. As the ruler faded from the public eye, it was the Gate that increasingly began to regulate procedures, imposing rules and regulations necessary to set various affairs in motion. Then one day the Gate issued an official statement detailing its jurisdiction, which extended over just about everything anyone could think of. This was the last document to bear the ruler's seal and signature. As time passed, the Gate began to introduce a few new policies, and soon it was the singular source of all regulations and decrees. Before long, it controlled absolutely everything, and made all procedures, paperwork, authorizations, and permits—even those for eating and drinking—subject to its control. It imposed costly fees on everything; even window-shopping was now subject to a charge, to be paid for by people out doing errands as well as those simply strolling down the sidewalk. To pay for the cost of printing all the documents it needed, the Gate deducted a portion of everyone's salary. This way it could ensure a system of the utmost efficiency, capable of implementing its philosophy in full.

A full range of security units soon appeared, too: the Deterrence Force existed to guard the Gate, and appeared only when something signaled danger near the building itself. The Concealment Force was tasked with protecting Zephyr Hospital and other facilities whose documents, files, and information were highly secret. Finally, the Quell Force handled direct confrontation and random skirmishes with protesters during times of unrest and chaos. It was well known that these guards were the least disciplined of all, yet also the fiercest in combat.

Yehya was no stranger to the string of disasters that the Gate's appearance had unleashed on the people. The company he worked for had nearly gone bankrupt after it was forced to pay new mandatory fees. Then a leaflet arrived, notifying the company that they'd been assigned with supplying equipment to the Alimentary Force. The task was prohibitively expensive and impossible to carry out without sustaining significant financial losses, and the company didn't even work in food services to begin with. But their appeals were returned to them stamped REJECTED. They were forced to lay off a number of employees to fulfill the assignment, and though Yehya survived the first round, he didn't expect to outlast the next. Murmurs of discontent circulated among the staff, but no one had the courage to speak up. It soon became clear that the Gate and its security units had tightened their grip throughout the region. The Gate's influence had begun to seep into businesses and organizations, onto the streets and into people's homes.

Then one day, Yehya heard about people who could no longer stand what was happening. Word spread that a small group of people, who had recently joined together, were going to organize a protest. He was skeptical that an uprising would be possible under the Gate's reign, but all the same he excused himself from work and left at the agreed-upon time, having decided to watch from afar. He had taken just a few steps in the direction of the square when he suddenly lost all sense of things—he realized he'd fallen to the ground, although he didn't feel any pain, and then he lost consciousness. He didn't wake up until he arrived at the hospital. Later, he learned that the Gate had closed that day in response to what became known as the Disgraceful Events. It hadn't opened since, nor had it attended to a single citizen's needs, yet it also hadn't stopped issuing laws and decrees. It had to open, Yehya figured. What reason did it have to remain closed? The Disgraceful Events had ended by affirming the Gate's hold on power and its growing omnipotence. Closing indefinitely made no sense, unless it was simply dealing out another form of punishment.

When they arrived at Amani's building, Nagy made his excuses and left so that Yehya could be alone with Amani. Yehya rang the bell a couple of times before Amani opened the door. Despite how deeply she had longed to see him, she looked into his eyes for just a fleeting moment before her gaze instinctively traveled downward. She scrutinized his clothes, and he quickly realized she was searching for any sign of bandages. Her face fell when she didn't see any, and she was filled again with a sense of anxiety. Though she hadn't believed in miracles since she was young, she kept wishing for one. She held fast to her hope that Yehya would undergo the operation: that it would succeed, he would recover, and this ridiculous nightmare they had been thrust into would end.

No matter what happened, Amani never changed. Yehya knew she was guided by her emotions and never considered things rationally. He knew she waited for her dreams to magically come true and never took obstacles into account, even if she was aware of them and how difficult they would be to overcome. He dealt with her optimism by trying to make reality match it as best he could, but this time was different. She'd been drawn into the incident herself. He pulled her close to him, putting an end to her inspection and wishful thinking. He kissed the top of her head and then her lips, but he couldn't hold her as he wanted to—the pain shot through his left side mercilessly, and he sat down, telling himself that there had to be better days ahead. She sat with him for a few minutes in the living room, then went to the kitchen and returned carrying two teacups and the cake she'd baked to celebrate his thirty-ninth birthday. He reflected with wry humor on the fact that it was the first birthday he'd celebrated with a bullet lodged in his guts.

She didn't have any candles in the apartment, and neither of them felt like acting out the usual celebrations anyway—it was enough just to be together. She poured them tea and cut the cake into generous helpings, wishing all the while that the bullet would simply disappear. She kissed him on the forehead and handed him his plate, but he couldn't eat with her; the stabbing pain had spread into his whole stomach and down his thighs. He lay down on the sofa and closed his eyes, and she brought him a glass of water and sat in a chair next to him, not daring to touch him. She was distraught. It tormented her to see him sprawled out like this, weak and defeated, and she felt so stupid and powerless. She knew that a glass of water wouldn't do anything to help. Yehya fell asleep and Amani wandered through her memories, pausing in front of the Northern Building where Yehya stood impatiently every day, waiting to enter. She'd seen the Northern Building often, but only ever from a distance: a strange crimson octagonal structure, slightly higher than the concrete walls that extended from it on either side. The main entrance to the building was the Gate itself, built into one of its eight sides. It had no visible windows or balconies, only barren walls of cast iron. If it weren't for the people who'd once entered it and told of all the rooms and offices inside, anyone gazing up at it would have imagined it to be a massive block, solid and impenetrable.

Yehya didn't sleep long. He was concerned when Amani fell silent and began to watch him attentively; she was counting his exhalations and synchronizing her breathing with his, so she would notice if anything changed. He gathered some strength and shifted on the sofa, and his face regained some life. It saddened him that they couldn't find anything else to talk about, just this bewildering mess that had become their sole subject of conversation from dawn until the ominous hours of the afternoon. He woke up and fell asleep and walked and ate and drank, and deep inside his body was a bullet that refused to leave him.

Yehya sat up, and when Amani saw this, some of the concern lifted from her face. She suggested they visit Tarek if there was still time; she was sure she could appeal to his sense of duty as a doctor and win him over, especially since things had changed since their last visit. Yehya had begun the necessary procedures: he had a place in the queue and would stay there until he received the permit. It was simply a matter of time now, nothing more, so maybe Tarek would show a little compassion and agree to help Yehya before all the paperwork was finished. There was no time for delay, or for adherence to arbitrary rules that weren't helping anyone. Yehya nodded, took a small bite of cake, and slowly stood up, clutching his side.

They were nearly out the door when the telephone rang, and Amani hesitated a moment before returning and picking it up. Nagy's baritone sprang out of the receiver, and he was pleased to hear her voice—it had been a long time since he'd seen her, maybe not since Yehya had been injured. He'd just finished his errands and was returning to the queue, and offered to walk Yehya back, but Amani asked him to meet them at the hospital instead. It was a chance to meet up after not having seen each other for a while, even if the place itself held bad memories for all three of them. Yehya took the phone from her to remind Nagy to be on his guard and watch his words if he arrived before them, to say nothing to Tarek about the other people waiting in the queue or why they were there. As Amani and Yehya walked down the stairs, she reminded him about the letter she'd sent him through Um Mabrouk; Yehya hadn't told her what he was going to do about the suspicious doctor who'd dropped by the office where they worked. Yehya realized with surprise that he'd completely forgotten about it. Her vague letter had confused and worried him when he received it, and he'd meant to ask her to explain what had happened. It held only one real piece of information: Zephyr Hospital, the place the man worked. Nothing aside from that, no name or rank or even his job title. The doctor hadn't asked her to do anything, not even to inform Yehya that he had come—he'd just asked Amani a brief question and then left. Although this enigmatic message was the reason Yehya had left the queue to visit Amani, it had evaporated from his memory, its place filled with pain. But again they put the discussion aside: it was getting late, and they hurried to catch Tarek.

Nagy took the quickest route he knew to the hospital. The streets practically looked like a carnival these days; ever since the Events had ended, they were overflowing with street vendors selling all kinds of food, drinks, clothes, and an array of everyday items. He enjoyed the lively, bustling atmosphere. Most important for him, it was a gold mine of books and papers. He noticed a wooden birdcage covered in a pile of newspapers and magazines in a dimly lit corner, and a man sitting cross-legged next to it, half asleep, his head drooping onto his shoulder as if he were about to wake at any moment. Nagy scanned the headlines, searching for something in particular. Without waking the man he left money for a copy of *The Truth* and a magazine—in theory a quarterly but now published only as often as its editors could manage. Hunger stirred in the depths of his belly, and he paused in front of a cart where sweet potatoes were roasted and sold. But the smoke rising from it brought back memories of those recent unsettling events. He stood there, frozen for a moment, and then quickly walked on, empty-handed but for the newspaper and magazine.

THREE

Document No. 3

Examinations Conducted, Visible Symptoms, and Preliminary Diagnosis

The patient is conscious, alert, and aware of his surroundings; blood pressure and pulse are normal; visible symptoms include: signs of choking and disruption of the nervous system, bleeding around entry and exit wounds caused by a [redacted], sign of recent abrasions and bruising on the back, pelvis, and forearm regions, [redacted; injury written above it] penetrating the pelvic region along with profuse bleeding, deviation of the wrist. Procedures conducted include [long sentence, redacted].

Required follow-up: Complete blood workup; kidney and liver function analysis; ultrasounds of the abdomen, pelvis, and chest; X-ray of the right forearm.

Tarek read the document again and again. Each time, he flipped the page over to check the other side, and each time he found it blank. He was searching for the detailed description he'd written and signed off himself after seeing the X-ray, but it wasn't there. There were pages missing; he didn't know how they had disappeared, but some other hand had clearly been meddling with the file. All the useful information had been crossed out and replaced with a superficial report; not even a fresh graduate would write something this worthless, and he hadn't any idea who had altered it.

He vividly remembered stopping the bleeding and performing a bit of first aid, and then being forced to close the wound, leaving the bullet where it was, next to Yehya's bladder. An act like that would never have occurred to him; he was a surgeon with a solid understanding of his work and an awareness of its repercussions. But a younger colleague had informed him that he would need a special permit if he intended to extract the bullet. After a heated debate, the other doctor went to the filing cabinet, took out a stack of papers that had been placed carefully on the top shelf, and pulled out a light-yellow document. He threw it down in front of Tarek, fed up with his naïveté, and told him to read it before making a decision. Tarek picked up the document and was struggling to understand it when a high-pitched whistle shot through their confrontation.

An ambulance had arrived and the injured patients were meticulously divided into groups, Yehya Gad el-Rab Saeed

41

among them. Their injuries were assessed, and then they were taken to the government-run Zephyr Hospital, which, according to announcements on the radio and TV, had gone above and beyond in its preparations for admitting the injured.

In his office now, Tarek left the file and folder on his desk and went to sit in the chair on the other side of the room, taking just the third document with him. This was the page that really bothered him, because every time he took it out of the file, began to read, and reached the end of the first paragraph, he remembered everything that had happened afterward. The morning after the Events, a doctor in military uniform appeared at the hospital and requested to meet him: him, Dr. Tarek Fahmy. The man refused to take a seat and turned down the cordial offers of tea or water while he was waiting. Tarek was summoned minutes later and tentatively approached to find a grave-looking doctor in his fifties pacing the lobby and pondering the imitation oil paintings hanging on the walls. Tarek invited him into his office and extended his hand, which the man shook coldly.

As soon as they shut the door behind them, the doctor produced the type of official ID that one didn't dare question, inquired about Yehya's X-ray, and then opened his briefcase and produced an order to confiscate it. Tarek asked if he would like some juice or something hot to drink, but the man firmly declined these, too. He stood up impatiently and asked Tarek for all existing copies of the X-ray. However, looking back, Tarek realized that the man hadn't actually asked questions. He hadn't phrased things in a way that left room for his request to be refused. The words that left his lips were direct orders, deftly coated with a sheen of courtesy but implying greater authority than any outpatient doctor possessed.

Tarek called the head nurse and told her to bring Yehya Gad el-Rab Saeed's file at once. The moment she knocked, the doctor grasped the handle, wrenched the door open, and snatched the file from her. Tarek stood there, his empty hand outstretched in her direction, where it remained suspended in the air for several seconds. The doctor told her to leave and not to disturb them, and shut the door again. In a leisurely way, he took a seat in Tarek's leather chair, engrossed in the X-ray and ignoring Tarek, who remained where he'd been standing in front of the door. The man took everything out of the file and then nodded, satisfied. He carefully removed the X-ray with a single word—"Excellent"—and then left the room.

Despite having suffered a nearly unbearable level of humiliation, Tarek kept silent until the man had left. Even if he'd been given a chance, he wouldn't have dared to object or question the doctor—he knew full well that the visit had something to do with the Gate of the Northern Building. Tarek would have been a fool to think there wouldn't be consequences if he crossed a man like that, especially in such difficult and uncertain times. A few hours later, he heard that the new X-ray machine in the basement had severely malfunctioned, and Sabah mentioned that she'd seen a Gate car with tinted windows take it away to be inspected and repaired. Yehya returned to the hospital two or three days later, utterly exhausted. The wound that Tarek had stitched up with his own hands was bleeding, and the man looked like he was about to pass out. Yehya introduced himself, though he didn't need to, and asked if Tarek could help him start the hospital-admittance procedures. He wanted to proceed with treatment to have the bullet removed, he said, and had left Zephyr Hospital to come here because the doctors there couldn't conduct the surgery he needed. After so many other injured people had arrived, they had told him his condition was relatively stable compared to the others, and had postponed the operation.

It made Tarek uneasy to remember how it hadn't felt like the right time to tell Yehya about the official visit he'd received from the doctor who had been interested specifically in his case, despite all the other injured patients. He knew he wouldn't be able to hide it forever; he knew Yehya would go looking for the X-ray when he came back, that one way or another he would discover it had been taken to Zephyr Hospital against his will, and that he wasn't likely to see it again. The scene that followed flashed through his mind: the empty room to which he'd helped Yehya walk, the door he'd made sure to close so no one could eavesdrop, the cabinet from which he'd taken the yellow document, the same one that had stopped him from performing the operation when Yehya had first arrived, injured. He recalled how the papers felt as he flipped through them for the first time so they could read what it said together, and he remembered the look on Yehya's face as he softly read aloud from the page in front of him:

Terms and Provisions Issued by the Gate on Conducting Work in Medical Facilities.

Article 4 (A): "Authorization for the Removal of Bullets." The extraction of a bullet or any other type of firearm projectile, whether in a clinic or a private or government hospital, from a body of a person killed or injured, is a criminal act, except when performed under official authorization issued by the Gate of the Northern Building; parties excluded from the above are limited to Zephyr

Hospital and its auxiliary buildings, which are direct sub-
sidiaries of the Gate.

Sanctions Imposed on Those in Violation of Article 4 (A):
Anyone who violates Article 4 (A), deliberately or inad-
vertently, shall be penalized as follows: First, s/he shall be
banned from practicing their profession; and Second, s/he
shall be imprisoned for a period to be determined by a
judge. After the period of his/her punishment has ended,
s/he shall not be allowed to return to the same position or
occupation, except after s/he undergoes a rehabilitation
program, the length of which shall be specially determined
by the Gate of the Northern Building; and s/he shall be
required to undergo a periodic performance review, at a
minimum of once every month, or more frequently, as the
situation requires.

There were a few lines written by hand in the margins, as if
someone reading it had added a couple of points that might
help the comprehension and implementation of the law. *"To
explain the article and its provisions—this measure has been taken
in response to current critical circumstances; as a rule, bullets and
projectiles may be the property of security units, and thus cannot
be removed from the body without special authorization."*

Sitting in his leather chair now, Tarek smiled. He remembered feeling the tension lift when he'd first absorbed that
passage and realized what fate he had narrowly escaped. He
had come so close to being investigated and interrogated, and
yet had unwittingly avoided it. Any shame he'd felt because of
Yehya had vanished; he had clearly taken the right course of
action. He had concealed his relief at the time, saying he was

deeply sorry and advising Yehya to wait his turn at Zephyr Hospital, then had jumped up and handed him some strong antibiotics and a few boxes of painkillers. He had walked Yehya to the door, promising to perform the surgery if Zephyr Hospital was still too crowded, just as soon as Yehya brought him a permit from the Gate. Yehya should come see him any-time, he said, any day of the week, there was no need to make an appointment.

Tarek would later learn that Yehya had indeed gone to the Gate. It was recorded in Document No. 5 in the file lying be-fore him on the desk, which stated that Yehya had arrived at the queue with a friend in early July, and while the date was not specified, the time was printed clearly at the top of the page: *9:25 a.m.*

THE CELL NETWORK DROPS

A middle-aged man gathered his nerves and decided to leave the queue without a word, just as Yehya and Nagy had done. He slipped away without making a fuss, but accidently left his newspaper and bag behind. He had already walked quite far and was about to get into a microbus when a stranger behind him in the queue noticed and called out to him, but with no luck. The stranger picked up the bag and rushed after the man, shouting, but the microbus sped away with the man inside, oblivious to the shouts and unaware that he had left his things behind. At a loss, the stranger returned to the queue and found that a group of people had gathered to watch the situation unfold. He opened the bag in front of them, but there was nothing in it that revealed the owner's identity. A ring of people formed around him. One onlooker said that the bag now belonged to the person who found it, but the man was too shy to agree with this suggestion and insisted that he wouldn't take it for himself.

The man in the *galabeya* intervened, assuring him there was nothing wrong with taking the bag, so long as he'd tried in good faith to return it to its owner. It was manna from heaven, he said, and what could be wrong with that? Things would have ended there were it not for a woman with short hair and a black skirt who had just arrived, looking for an empty place closer to the Gate. She joined the little gathering and proposed

that they keep the bag for a day or two, and if its owner—
who would likely come back looking for it—hadn't returned by
then, it would be best to hand it over to the official sitting in
a nearby booth, or to the guard posted nearby. That way no
one could say they'd done anything wrong or taken something
that didn't belong to them. Her presence among them irritated
the man in the *galabeya*. He turned away from her sanctimo-
niously, and she heard him mutter a prayer for busybodies to
be led toward the right path, and the same for fools and the
ignorant, who know not the difference between righteousness
and sin. A few people sided with him, disgruntled that she'd
interjected, and a clean-shaven man, averting his gaze, asked
whether it was right to listen to the opinion of a woman standing so immodestly among a group of men. He didn't wait for
a response, and placing his hand on the shoulder of the man
with the bag—who was becoming increasingly distressed at the
center of a rapidly growing audience—he told him to empty
it out so everyone else could divide its contents among themselves, and thus keep any one of them from falling into sin.

Ines found herself standing at the edge of a crisis erupting
just a few feet away from her. While it troubled her to see the
woman being attacked, she remained where she was, trying to
stay out of the argument. But as insult after insult was hurled
upon the woman, who stood her ground and tried to protect
the bag, Ines couldn't take it anymore, and moving closer to
the circle, she shouted: "She's right." Her voice emerged feeble
and faint, yet loud enough that they all turned around. The
man in the *galabeya* stared at her for a long time without responding. However brief, her words had unambiguously allied
her with the other woman. It was clear that an opposing side
was forming.

Ines felt her face grow red as a wave of embarrassment passed over her; her interjection had halted the discussion, and curious faces began to inspect her as if waiting for her to utter something further. Finally Ehab, that journalist who often hung around, intervened. He offered to take the bag to the newspaper headquarters where he worked, make an inventory of what was in it, and publish a small notice with a description. Maybe the owner would recognize the bag, and he would probably rather pick it up from the newspaper office than go to the Booth near the Gate. A few people opposed Ehab's suggestion, but the rest agreed with him, and so Ines returned to her place in one piece, while the woman with the short hair continued her search for somewhere to stand.

The queue grew calm as the disc of sun slipped down behind the Gate. The period of rest had begun, the hour when Hammoud always arrived with drinks. A few people performed their evening prayers, while others sat cross-legged on the ground, waiting for tea and *yensoon*, the hot anise drink. But the boys from the coffee shop didn't arrive. Time dragged on. After a whole hour went by from the time they usually came, people began to fidget and grumble, and finally someone called out to the microbus driver, asking if he knew where the boys were. The driver told him there was construction going on near the coffee shop, and all the boys were busy serving the workers. Ehab tried calling Hammoud on the phone (he was keen to discuss the day's updates and stories from the queue, and record their conversation), but without success. Then he tried to call a colleague at the newspaper, but his phone couldn't get any signal. He took the battery out, put it back in, and tried again: no luck. He started to walk around, and soon discovered that he was not the only one having problems.

It began gradually, affecting just a few others, then dozens, then hundreds, and the numbers kept rising, until people finally realized it was a system-wide outage. Amid the confusion, the man in the *galabeya* strolled toward Ines, fiddling with his prayer beads and pretending not to be heading straight for her. She was startled when he stopped just a couple of steps away, his wide eyes staring right at her. He bade her the full, formal religious greeting with a reedy voice that was so incongruous with his sullen visage that she just barely stopped herself from laughing out loud. She returned the greeting hesitantly, consciously lowering her gaze, as was proper. He offered to let her use his cell phone, which still worked despite the outage, in case her family was worried or would want to know where she was. She thanked him, surprised, but there was no one she needed to call—her parents wouldn't be back from the Gulf for another two months, and her sister, who was married, would still be working at the preschool at this hour. She didn't know what made her open up to him and share such personal information, but he stroked his beard contentedly and told her she could use his phone whenever she wanted. He went back to his place in the queue but not before casting a fleeting glance at her hands; he was pleased with her tender skin and the absence of a ring.

THE NIGHT OF JUNE 18

The hospital where Tarek worked wasn't far, but Amani insisted that Yehya shouldn't walk there when he was so tired. They flagged down a taxi, each thinking about what the meeting might bring.

Yehya went over the events in his mind, so that he wouldn't slip up when talking to Tarek. When he had arrived at Zephyr Hospital on the night of June 18, there had been dozens of people like him, maybe even hundreds. There were some with three or four bullets lodged in their bodies and others with less-serious injuries. When they postponed his operation, Yehya complained to the nurses for two whole days, but he quickly changed his tune on the third, when a medical report was released about the other patient in his room. The man lay there in a coma with a bullet in his head; Yehya had actually seen him get shot. But the report claimed that the man had suffered an epileptic fit and somehow fallen from a great height onto a solid metal object, injuring his head and thus passing into a coma. Furthermore, the report emphasized that no bullets had been visible on the man's X-ray. Around noon, Yehya heard the same thing reported about two other patients who had just left the operating room. Later that day, he borrowed a phone from the father of the patient in the room with him, called Amani, and asked her to come and visit him sooner than they'd arranged. In clipped words, he conveyed

51

that strange things were happening and that he no longer felt comfortable staying there. He wasn't sure whether they would operate on him to remove his bullet, which perhaps had also inexplicably disappeared.

On the fourth day after he was injured, he called Amani again and learned that she hadn't been able to enter the hospital because of its complex security procedures. These were imposed to "ensure patient comfort," she had been informed. She also told him that the Gate had released a statement claiming that no bullets had been fired at the place and time at which he had been injured. Several prominent journalists published full-page articles concurring that no bullets had been found, neither in the bodies of the dead nor of the injured. Eyewitnesses they quoted insisted that the people who caused the Disgraceful Events were just rioters who had suddenly "lost all moral inhibitions" and flown into a frenzy: first they insulted one another, then they threw stones, and finally they seized iron bars from an old, vacant building belonging to the Gate. Any injuries they sustained were simply puncture wounds they suffered while struggling over the bars they'd wrenched off.

On the phone, Amani read him a statement in *The Truth* newspaper made by an anonymous doctor supervising the treatment of the wounded at Zephyr Hospital. The doctor asserted that the high mortality rate was due to the fact that these rioters were simply too sensitive. Upon hearing one another's harsh words, they'd succumbed automatically, their hearts having stopped before the ambulances even arrived. Others had stumbled upon the grisly scene and were so traumatized by it that they froze, and then they collapsed, too, falling one after another like dominoes. Some journalists went even further and published unconfirmed reports that the people who died were not in fact killed but had committed suicide when they saw what had happened. They even claimed that one of them had stabbed several others with an iron stake before turning it upon himself, Japanese seppuku-style. At this point, Yehya made a decision. He slipped away from his bed unnoticed and returned alone to the hospital where Tarek worked. When he arrived, he caught a glimpse of the doctor in the lobby, but was suddenly overwhelmed with fatigue and forgot the doctor's name. He gestured toward him inquiringly, and a nurse responded automatically, without even glancing at the rotations sheet: Dr. Tarek Fahmy.

Back in the taxi, Yehya remembered the papers that Tarek had shown him in the hospital that day and let out a sigh. At first he couldn't believe they were real, and looked carefully through the whole pile. But when he saw the Gate's stamp on the back of every page, he realized that there was nothing he could do. He'd left the hospital and spent the first night lying by the side of the road. He felt hopeless: he couldn't ask any friend or acquaintance for help. He didn't have his phone on him, he couldn't even walk, and no passing car would give him a lift because his injury looked so suspicious that helping him would put them in danger. The next day he begged a sympathetic stranger to let him use his phone, and was able to reach Nagy, who brought him home. Nagy stayed with him for days, how many exactly Yehya didn't know, until the bleeding had stopped and the wound had closed, trapping the bullet in his pelvis. Then Nagy had gone with him to the Gate for the first time in their lives.

The car stopped on a quiet street, and Yehya snuffed out his memories. He paid the driver and stepped out of the taxi. Yehya walked through the hospital door with Amani by his side at precisely six in the evening, when Tarek's shift began. They saw that Nagy had beaten them there, as they'd expected he would, and taken up a prime reconnaissance position that enabled him to see everyone who came in and out of the lobby. Sabah appeared apprehensive when she saw them. She was standing by the information desk, chatting happily with a colleague, and as they walked in, she stopped midsentence, revealing that she knew exactly who he was. He remembered her quite well, too, from his two previous visits to the hospital: her round face lined with care. She tried to act normal, greeting him with her customary phrase for all visitors, and asked him some standard questions as if he were one of the scores of new patients she saw every day. But the expression on her face betrayed her unease, and her words came out shaky and jumbled, her voice wavering. "I'll look for him," she said, as she rushed off toward Tarek's office. "But, of course, Dr. Tarek might have left, he never works nights."

SABAH

The first time Sabah had seen Yehya was the night of the Disgraceful Events, as he was carried into the emergency room. She took him in, put an IV in the back of his hand to administer blood and fluids, and then left to help other patients while Tarek dealt with his injuries and observed his general state of health. That same night, at exactly 3:30 a.m., after all the patients had been transferred, Sabah received a personal call from a senior doctor at Zephyr Hospital, an influential man. He told her not to ask questions, but to go to the filing department, remove Yehya Gad el-Rab Saeed's medical file, read it to him, and then alter some of the language to match what he had personally observed in the patient. The doctors and nurses were all overwhelmed with fatigue and the horror of what they had seen that day. Everyone went to lie down the first chance they got, and those who weren't on the night shift headed home to sleep, as they all expected the events to continue the following day.

Sabah didn't have much choice; the discussion was over in seconds. She was just a junior nurse there, young and insignificant, while the man on the other end was extremely senior, in age and position. Senior enough, perhaps, to fire her from this job and any other she might find, senior enough to shut down the entire hospital.

After things calmed down somewhat, when the night owls

began to quiet and security measures waned, Sabah was able to sneak off and carry out the orders she had been given, fully and precisely. The second time she saw Yehya was an unlucky coincidence. He ran into her in the lobby, half-conscious and disoriented, asking for Tarek but not by name. Yehya didn't spend long with him, and he left shortly afterward. She'd forgotten all about him, but now here he was, appearing before her for the third time like a ghost.

Nagy put the newspaper aside and joined his friends. Amani sat across from the corridor to the doctors' offices, while Yehya leaned back against the wall, trying to stave off the pain by staying still as much as possible. He'd grown used to standing in the queue for hours on end, and now could stay like that for a whole day without his feet tiring or troubling him.

When Tarek arrived, he was as flustered as Sabah had been; he hurried toward them and then stopped in front of them, clearly nervous. He didn't reach out for a handshake until Amani did.

"I'm Amani, a colleague of Yehya's," she said, offering her hand. "I brought him here when he was injured."

Tarek gave her a quick smile, one that was not welcoming, and led them to his office. Nagy signaled that he would stay where he was. Tarek asked Sabah to bring them tea, and then firmly closed the door behind them.

"Yehya, hello. How are you feeling?"

"I'm good, Doctor, the wound is healing, but it still hurts. It feels like the bullet is moving around in there."

"They haven't done the operation yet? You must be here with authorization from the Gate, then, so we can schedule a suitable time?"

"Well, actually, I've finished part of the procedure—I submitted an application to the Booth with all the necessary paperwork, and now I'm just waiting to be granted the permit."

Although she was annoyed by how formal and unfeeling the conversation was, Amani joined in with a sweet, pleasant smile, and a tone she tried to make as friendly as possible.

"Dr. Tarek, do you think we could start preparing for the operation while we're waiting for the permit? Everything's in order, we just have to go through the motions now."

"I'll be completely honest with you," Tarek said. "I've done everything I can, and Yehya knows that, but we simply cannot take any steps that have any connection to the operation without proper authorization."

Amani's smile became strained, and she leaned forward in her chair as if by moving closer to Tarek she could convince him.

"But from what the doctors at Zephyr Hospital said, and from what you yourself told Yehya right here, he's in real danger. The longer he waits, the more likely the bullet might tear through his intestines, and you wouldn't be able to stop the bleeding or do anything about it—isn't that what you said?"

"The matter is out of my hands, I'm afraid—if I could have done the operation, I would never have postponed it in the first place. The new laws and decrees state that one must have authorization, and it's impossible to act against the official instructions we receive from the Gate. You both know how it is."

Amani's smile evaporated. She raised her voice, reminding him he was a doctor, that his first priority was to help the sick, and he shot back that helping the sick was subject to the law, too; it wasn't just every man for himself. Yehya intervened before things developed into an all-out shouting match, and gestured to Amani to calm down before turning to Tarek.

"It's no problem at all, Dr. Tarek. Hopefully I'll be back

here with the authorization in a few days. If I could just ask you for the X-ray you took—when the Gate opens, I'll probably need it as proof of my situation."

Just moments before, Tarek had been able to defend himself with a logical explanation that they couldn't argue with, but now his voice caught in his throat. Here it was: they had finally arrived at what had kept him awake through countless nights, but still he hadn't figured out what he was going to say. He stood there, backed up against the desk, stuck there with no way forward and no way out. A sudden thought flashed into his mind; he could say no X-rays were performed in the hospital that day, but then he realized that he had told Yehya everything he'd seen in the X-ray himself. True, the notes he had written down had now vanished, and the X-ray technician no longer had any evidence because the negatives had been seized. And true, no specialist would have had time to write up an independent report due to the chaos and crowds that had engulfed the hospital that night . . . but Tarek himself knew it had been performed, that it had been here in Yehya's file, and that Yehya had a right to see it.

He couldn't lie so brazenly, even if he wanted to. He couldn't deny what had happened and stand by it. He may have been weak and a coward, but he wasn't a liar. He'd failed at dealing with problems like this his whole life, though he saw his colleagues doing it all the time, inventing a lie here and another one there, weaving thoroughly fabricated excuses. They often offered to help him do the same, to get out of a predicament or shirk responsibilities, but he never could.

He decided to tell them the truth, and whatever happened, happened, but two knocks on the door interrupted his tumultuous thoughts. Sabah entered the room carrying tea, and before she left he suddenly found himself telling her to bring Yehya's X-ray from the head nurse. It was no innocent request; the head nurse had gone on a long vacation, and her absence provided a plausible opportunity to postpone the whole situation. It would give him a bit more time to think things over again, when he wasn't under such pressure, and come up with a plan. Amani was making him nervous, and the two of them would likely be back. Tarek knew how important the X-ray was for Yehya, and he didn't want to end the matter so much as he wanted to find a solution whereby no one would get hurt. What exactly should he divulge now, and what should he hide, without being forced to resort to a barefaced lie?

Everything went relatively smoothly. Sabah returned and, with a glance at Tarek, said the head nurse wasn't in, she was out on some errands. Amani grew tense at the hackneyed excuse and pursed her lips, while Yehya maintained his composure, his calm expression tinged with a hint of frustration. Tarek (who for his part had strived to put on a believable performance) appeared just as surprised as they did. He let out an apologetic sigh and mustered an expression he hoped conveyed disappointment. He didn't know whether he'd managed to convince them, but after a moment he truly did feel sorry for Yehya.

Perhaps it was the air of despondency that descended upon them, or the tension that threatened to ignite an argument between him and Amani all over again. Whichever it was didn't matter; the quandary in which they'd found themselves forced him to keep thinking until he found the perfect way out. He remembered that when patients were transferred to other hospitals for further treatment, copies of their X-rays and medical tests were automatically sent with them. If Yehya's had been sent to one of the government-run or military hospitals, getting it from there would certainly be difficult, but it was worth a shot. He cracked his knuckles and declared that there was no need to wait for the head nurse, it was better for them to act now. Worst-case scenario, they could try to find a copy of the X-ray in the Department of Personal Medical Files at Zephyr Hospital, which he'd heard was in the basement.

Yehya shook off the sense of apathy that had settled over him, and interest flickered across his face. He stared at Tarek for a moment. "The basement?" he asked. He'd heard it mentioned before. Yehya leaned his head back and closed his eyes. Memories of his first trip to the Gate with Nagy played in his mind, the task they hadn't managed to accomplish because at the time neither of them had known how things were done. He'd been told that in order to submit an application for a permit, he first needed to go to the Booth, a small structure on the side of the Northern Building. There he needed to hand in his paperwork and state the purpose of his request. The official there would check that his papers were in order, file the application, and give him a stamped receipt as confirmation. Only individuals who had gone to the Booth to register and inform the Gate of their purpose were entitled to wait in the queue. The Booth itself was able to process certain preliminary paperwork, like applications for Certificate of True Citizenship, but decisions on permit applications could come only from the Gate and only when it opened.

Yehya had left Nagy and made his way there, following the instructions he'd been given until he arrived at the building, which was immensely tall and seemed uninhabited. At the base of the Northern Building was a small boxlike hut, with barely enough room for the official inside, who was sitting at the counter behind a small, high window with iron bars. In front there was a small, solitary sign with the words *The Booth* written in a sharp hand, and in the far right corner was the local calligrapher's peculiar signature: *Abbas.*

To reach the window, Yehya had needed to stand on his tiptoes, which was difficult, and he felt a tearing sensation in his side, as the wound was still tender. He passed his papers through the iron bars and asked the official if he would need to keep them until the Gate opened. The official's face soured before Yehya had even finished his sentence. He snatched the papers violently and perused them with intrigue, then carefully examined Yehya's face without responding. Yehya repeated the question. An old man who stood there filling out a long convoluted form seemed to take pity on him, and with a cautious glance around them, he whispered in Yehya's ear that the Booth was actually connected to the Gate, by a long tunnel that led all the way to the basement. Regardless of when the Gate opened, his papers would be in the bowels of the building soon, added to his file and subject to careful examination.

Back in Tarek's office, Yehya stood up to leave. Amani rushed to help him, while Tarek stood there watching them curiously, as if reconsidering his medical evaluation of the case. Their cups of tea sat untouched, but they thanked him for his time and Amani asked him to let them know as soon as the head nurse returned, adding that she would call him if anything changed.

They found Nagy stretched out in a chair with his eyes closed, and Amani gently shook his shoulder. His eyes snapped open, and then he closed them again and sluggishly stood up. A few minutes later they arrived at a deserted microbus stop. Nagy broke the silence, suggesting that Yehya stay at his place for the night and rest up after such an exhausting day. Yehya quickly agreed, indulging in the hope of a quiet night to consider the possibilities in front of him. But Amani barely heard them; her mind was fixed on one thing. Suddenly she announced that she would go to Zephyr Hospital and submit a request for the X-ray. Yehya objected instantly, opposed to the idea of her going to that place by herself; just the thought of it made him anxious. His own experience there was not at all encouraging, and Amani knew what had happened to him there, but Nagy supported her. He told Yehya to stop and think about it, to put his feelings aside and listen to reason. Amani was far less likely to raise suspicion, for a reason that was obvious to all of them: Yehya was clearly injured, and that was impossible to hide.

Yehya went straight back to the queue the next morning, only to find someone in his place. The newcomer had arrived and insisted that Ines let him stand behind her given his circumstances, as he was in a rush to finish what he came for and return to his hometown. He had asked her with deep reverence and conviction, as he gazed up at the sky: if he were not fated for that spot, why would God have compelled him to walk from the end of the queue all the way to her? Ines hadn't been particularly bothered by Yehya's presence behind her over the past several days, yet neither was she especially grateful for it. She wasn't overly interested in him. He kept to himself, not joining anyone—other than his friend—in anything, neither friendly conversation nor fights. He'd spoken to her only once and hadn't even bothered to tell her that he was leaving or when he would be back. She hesitated momentarily to wrestle with her conscience—she didn't think it was right to hand over a place in the queue so easily—but after another moment, she gestured at the place and shrugged disinterestedly. With her consent, Shalaby took Yehya's place, making sure to stamp his footprint in the ground, and then stood there, delighted with his own resourcefulness. He cast a proud glance at the horizon, which was brimming with people behind him. The queue grew longer and longer every day, and the space it took up grew ever wider. He noticed that while only a few people left and didn't return, new waves arrived every day, stretching the queue ever farther. He had even heard rumors, later revealed to be untrue, that it had crossed into the neighboring governorate.

Yehya didn't blame Ines; after all, it had been Shalaby's idea, and she had only reluctantly given in. He didn't think there was any point in speaking to Shalaby, either, since he stood there with such bravado, obstructing the place like a concrete pillar. Luck had never been on Yehya's side, even from the start, and he turned away, head hanging low. He slowly squeezed himself into an Upper Line microbus, a kind he hadn't taken before. Nagy had told him that the Upper Line was just one of several lines created recently, because one day, without any discussion, everyone had begun to drive on the sidewalks, abandoning the roads to the people in the queue. Three hours later he arrived at the back of the queue and took up a new place at the very end. Once there, he cast a long look at the Gate. From afar, it looked like a solid wall, and he wondered in despair whether it would ever open.

THE GATE OF MALADIES

Amani answered the phone; the network was back up. Her voice caught in her throat, shaky and choked, and at first Nagy thought she was ill. He realized that she was on the way to the former District 3 to give her condolences to Um Mabrouk, whose elder daughter had died. Her heart had given out one day, after she had waited years to replace its malformed valves. He realized that it wasn't a good time and quickly ended the conversation, asking her to call him back when the funeral was over.

Amani sobbed harder as she approached Um Mabrouk's apartment, imagining Yehya dying. She pictured his funeral procession, and mourners departing from the queue to join it, and then burying him in a mass grave for victims of the Disgraceful Events, all without the bullet ever being removed.

She arrived in the courtyard with red, swollen eyes, her face drained and pale. Um Mabrouk was sitting by the front door, barefoot and wearing a black headscarf tied behind her head. Her neighbors sat around her, crying and comforting her, making coffee and tea, and sharing memories about the girl. Um Mabrouk stood up when she saw Amani coming, leaned on the women for support, and then rushed toward her. They hugged for a long time while Um Mabrouk sobbed, begging those around her to agree about how hard she had it, and then she began to console Amani, who was crying even harder, suddenly overwhelmed by the terrifying scenes in her imagination and the feeling of being completely alone. Um Mabrouk thanked her for having taken the trouble to come, grateful because she thought Amani might have been too exhausted, given the situation.

"Don't worry, Amani, don't work yourself up like this. She really loved you . . . but it's all in God's hands. Death comes for us all, in the end."

Amani stayed until the mourners dispersed and all the neighbors went home. She felt heavy in her seat and couldn't bring herself to leave. Finally, Um Mabrouk began to climb the stairs to bed, along with her husband, who had appeared at the last minute, and she offered to let Amani spend the night if she wanted. It wasn't until then that Amani finally managed a few words of condolence and said goodbye.

Um Mabrouk needed to use the death of her elder daughter as leverage to save the younger one, so she gathered the death certificate and all the tattered reports she'd saved since her daughter was a child and made the rounds of her acquaintances, asking for the funds she needed to get help. She wouldn't leave until she told them of the misfortune that had befallen her and the second tragedy that lay ahead, and she asked for help from all her neighbors, even Amani's doorman. Yet despite her efforts, she didn't manage to collect enough money for the operation. She knocked on the hospital director's door more than once, and when she couldn't find him there she waited next to his official car. She bent down and kissed his hand as soon as he appeared, pleading with him to waive just half the fee, but he shook her off with disdain and directed her to the Gate of Maladies, which presided over such cases.

The Gate of Maladies had been built a long time ago, and Um Mabrouk hadn't been there since she was just a child, prone to illness. A doctor had warned her mother not to ignore Um Mabrouk's chronically inflamed tonsils, so she took her to a public hospital to have them removed. The doctor there told her to go to the Gate of Maladies, a new ministry that now had jurisdiction over the hospital. There, he promised, she could sign up for free treatment. The Gate of Maladies was clean and tidy when they arrived—not many people had yet set foot inside—and she registered her name. But her turn never came. In the end, she had to go to a private doctor; he lowered his fee for her, and her mother borrowed the rest. He removed her tonsils, the matter ended, and she hadn't been back to the Gate of Maladies since.

The Gate of Maladies was founded decades before the Gate of the Northern Building, and there wasn't much overlap in their jurisdiction. The Gate of Maladies acted as a liaison between citizens who had complaints about their health care and the doctors and officials responsible for them; it delivered petitions and collected responses, but it never actually prosecuted anyone for wrongdoing. It took a year or two or even more for the Gate of Maladies to begin the paperwork needed to take action, and there were crumbling papers in its old chambers that had been waiting for decades to be finalized. Some, the descendants of the plaintiffs followed up on, while others were kept in trust, never to be discarded, even if no one ever asked about them again.

Um Mabrouk didn't waste any time: she confirmed that the Gate of Maladies still stood where she remembered it to be and then headed there, following the hospital director's instructions. Inside an office on the ground floor, an official took a quick glance at her papers and pursed his lips. She wouldn't receive a Treatment Permit for her second daughter unless she amended the application form, he said, and her first daughter's death certificate as well. Um Mabrouk pleaded with him, opening her wallet to show she barely had enough to survive as it was; a few measly pounds was all the money she had in the world. She followed this with a prayer to keep his family and children from harm, making sure then to reveal the fifty-pound note she'd brought hoping it would satisfy him. But he pursed his lips again and told her that the cause of death written on her daughter's death certificate was *inappropriate*. The girl died because her time was up, he said; she couldn't expect doctors to alter fate. Even if medicine could perform miracles, the doctors couldn't have extended her daughter's life, not even by a moment. "You *do* believe in God, don't you, *ya Hagga?*" he asked. She said nothing, and he carried on, telling her there was no need to go around blaming other people for her own woes. Finally, she asked him for his advice. His expression softened. He invited her to make herself comfortable on the broken wooden chair sitting in front of his desk, and then leaned in closer. He whispered in her ear that to obtain a Treatment Permit, she had to fill out a new application, praising the care her dearly departed daughter had received before her time was up. Then she must go to the Gate of the Northern Building and change the cause of death to something more *appropriate*. Finally, she had to withdraw the complaint she had submitted about her elder daughter's death, and the documents she'd attached to prove that her living daughter's condition had deteriorated. And, since she didn't have enough money to pay for it, she had to take her daughter off the wait list for surgery.

He gave her an application form that was already filled out, and she signed her name at the bottom of the page and gave it back to him to keep in the file. He told her not to worry about providing her fingerprints—she'd been so cooperative—and then he handed her more paperwork for the Gate. He assured her that obtaining a new death certificate would go smoothly now, and told her the Gate would provide her with a new copy that day since there would be no need to cross-check it. Pretending to be confused and in a rush, she let her fifty-pound note fall into the folder on his desk and turned to go, and didn't hear a word from him as she walked out the door.

Yehya received an endless stream of news from his new position in the queue, which was no longer at the end, as it had been when he first got there, because dozens more people had since arrived behind him. Ehab brought news of an opinion poll conducted by the Center for Freedom and Righteousness, under the Gate's supervision of course. They had dispatched droves of delegates to knock on people's doors during dawn prayer time, to ask their opinion of recent events and how the country was being run. The results had finally been released, and were precisely the same as the results of the previous poll. Citizens had unanimously endorsed its governance, laws, and court rulings—wholeheartedly and dutifully supporting the just decrees that had recently been issued. Those conducting the poll had therefore decided not to conduct one again. To simplify matters, they would announce the previous poll's results on a set yearly date.

A leaflet from the Violet Telecom Company arrived too, announcing a great promotion for all citizens: thousands of free phone lines and endless credit for an entire year. The leaflet said that the company would hold a lottery every two weeks to select ten winners, and would send them new phones, too, equipped with all the latest features and services, with no restrictions or terms and conditions. This piece of news was met with particular delight by everyone waiting in the queue and they considered it a fitting apology for the strange fact that the network had been down recently. Rumors also spread—though they could not be confirmed—that Upper Line and Normal Line microbuses would be forbidden to carry passengers for a few days, and that stations would be closed to conserve fuel.

A few people in the know speculated that this meant there was a need for more diesel fuel to clean up the square and the surrounding streets, and to remove the stains and traces left by the Disgraceful Events. Others said that some of the fuel would be dumped down the sewage drains, under a comprehensive national plan aimed at eradicating the insects that had spread throughout the country in swarms. These appeared to be breeding primarily around the queue, due to the crowding and unsanitary conditions. Most people scoffed at the last rumor, yet there had been an undeniable decline in the numbers of microbuses, which led some to believe it. Still, the microbus service had never before been completely suspended.

There was no shortage of reports on when the Gate would open, and this was the greatest source of chaos and contention. People at the end of the queue swapped stories that the Gate had already opened, while those stuck in the middle said they had a week ahead of them at most. Other stubborn rumors, whose provenance no one knew, said that the people standing at the front had heard voices coming from behind the Gate: whole conversations, the rustling of papers, the clatter of cups and spoons. But when these rumors finally reached the people at the front, they said they'd only seen shadows, arriving and departing, but that the gate hadn't opened and no one had ever actually appeared.

Um Mabrouk arrived at the queue with a big cloth sack containing a threadbare sheet, a small plastic mat, a round of flatbread with an egg inside, still in its shell, and the stack of papers the official at the Booth had given her without telling her what to do with them. She'd begun to set up camp when she was suddenly struck with the sense that she would be here for a long time, though how long she didn't know. Meanwhile, Nagy hurried to meet Yehya in his new place in the queue. Nagy had just submitted an application to the Translation Office, after seeing the same job advertisement published in a small box in *The Truth* for several weeks on end. The advertisement didn't request any specific skills; it just called for all humanities graduates to apply, regardless of their language abilities.

But a soldier stopped the Upper Line microbus that Nagy was riding toward the Gate, and forced the driver to turn around at the next street. The area was off-limits now, so Nagy got off and was forced to go the rest of the way on foot. When he arrived, Ehab told him that the road to the queue and even all the sidewalks were closed to cars in both directions, and that the Gate had issued a decree on the matter, recently broadcast in one of its frequent and confusing messages. In a low voice the others couldn't hear, Ehab added that the decision would soon apply to pedestrians, too— you'd only be allowed to walk toward the Gate, not away from it. And as soon as the Gate began to receive people, you would only be able to exit on the far side, which wasn't visible from where they were standing, nor from anywhere in the queue. This way, no citizen who completed his paperwork would be able to disobey instructions, turn around with his papers, and walk in the opposite direction.

Over the weeks that followed, Um Mabrouk gradually moved up the queue by providing all sorts of key services. She cleaned people's things, played with their children, did their grocery shopping, and sometimes even washed their clothes. She finally settled near Ines in a place to her liking and had no problems mixing with everyone else. She resumed her normal activities, but soon became more interested in the rumors and scattered bits of news she heard now and then. One day, she declared that the insect infestation people were discussing was just "*nifs*" and had nothing to do with how clean the place was. Ines asked her what she meant, and she explained that the insects were a result of the evil eye: other people outside the queue clearly had ill will toward everyone gathered in front of the Gate. People kept arriving at the queue, and the numbers continued to rise, so much so that they would soon block out the sun. But despite how crowded it was, the people in the queue lived their lives and solved their own problems without help from anyone. This was exactly what made people outside the queue fear and envy them, and what set their schemes in motion. They didn't want the people in the queue to be a united collective or "one hand." Um Mabrouk added that such things often happened in the alley where she lived; people everywhere needed to keep jealousy and the evil eye at bay. Ines said nothing, but Shalaby—whose arrogance had not diminished since his arrival—confidently agreed with her.

71

SHALABY

It didn't take long for Shalaby to creep into their conversation, gradually at first, with a few well-placed comments. Then, when neither Um Mabrouk nor Ines objected, he picked up the thread of the discussion and refused to let go. He seemed to have been waiting for an opportunity to enter the tight cliques that had formed among veterans of the queue. These were difficult to penetrate, so newcomers created their own circles of camaraderie. Shalaby hadn't been able to join a single one of those, either, though not for lack of effort.

With Um Mabrouk and Ines he found a new beginning, a way to announce his presence and loosen his tongue, which had nearly stuck to the roof of his mouth because of how long he'd gone without talking. His mother used incense to ward off the evil eye, he began, though he himself preferred to read the incantations he'd memorized as a five-year-old, when his father sat him and his cousin Mahfouz down to teach them everything they needed to know about life. He eagerly pre-empted any questions: no, he personally had no need for the Gate; it was Mahfouz, God rest his soul, who was the reason he'd come here from his village, though he'd sworn to himself he would never leave it again. He'd finished his service a couple of months back, and gone home to his village to settle down and raise a family in his father's house, and to begin to deal with the land issues that had multiplied in his absence.

He and Mahfouz were around the same age; they'd been raised together, had fallen sick with measles together, and had left elementary school together to work in the fields. That was until all the farmable land around their village dried up and the landowner began to quarrel with their families over the few meager acres they leased and lived off. So he and Mahfouz started shift work at Fino Bakery instead, then worked as plumbers, installing shower pipes, and finally were conscripted when they both came of age. Shalaby was selected to be a guard in the Servant Force, assigned to protect the wife and children of a Middle Sector Commander, and thus relieved from more difficult duties, while Mahfouz was chosen for the Quell Force. It was Mahfouz's sworn duty to protect and defend the country from Godless infidels, unscrupulous rebels, and other filth who were bent on destruction and had an insatiable appetite for dirty money.

Mahfouz never dawdled when given an order, and because of his massive frame, the Commander positioned him in the advance guard. In every clash and battle, he stood there, an impregnable fortress, and not once did anyone break through the wall that was Mahfouz's solid body. These were the stories his fellow guards told, but they also said he was dutiful and kind; he never quarreled or complained, he sang the Commander's praises day and night, and his only response to orders was "*Yessir.*" He cleaned the army vehicles, cooked meals in the mess hall, and fixed the electricity: he knew why it cut out and how to repair it, thanks to his early years in the village. He advanced when given the command, struck as soon as he heard the signal, and never paid heed to rumors. He was a model member of the security forces and thoroughly dependable.

Shalaby carried on boasting about his cousin, extolling his

merits and telling tales of his heroism, unaware of Ines's growing restlessness and Um Mabrouk's expression, which swung
between envious admiration and cautious disbelief. Finally,
Shalaby's eyes filled with sadness as he gazed at the ground
and said: But Mahfouz died. His truncheon crashed down on
a filthy rioter's damn head, but the stubborn scum kept trying
to get up so Mahfouz shot him. His blood gushed out and
stained the square, and his soul left his body right there. The
man's friends chased Mahfouz for ages and none of his fellow
guards could help him, because the battle had gotten so cha-
otic. They surrounded him on the bridge, there were so many
of them and he was all alone, so he jumped into the water,
afraid they would catch him, and drowned.

Mahfouz's name didn't appear on the list of Righteous
Guards released by the Gate; but he must have been omitted
accidentally, because his superiors and Commander certainly
recognized him as a hero. Shalaby proudly announced that
he'd come to request honorable recognition for Mahfouz, and
a Special Pension Permit for the grieving family who should
be appropriately compensated, with, for example, a contract
giving them the land the owner was threatening to evict them
from. Shalaby fell silent for a moment, then declared that his
cousin deserved to be named a war hero—no, a martyr!—
which was also what the man he'd killed deserved to be called.

Yet amid his tales, Shalaby didn't mention—because of respect for the dead, his own reserve, and the idyllic image he
had proudly painted—that Mahfouz had made a mistake or
two. The last time was when the world turned upside down
and he was tasked with guarding a hospital. Mahfouz said
he'd struck a deal with a patient suffering from a bad liver
to spend the night with her. But then she screamed out in

fear, and when the doctors and nurses on duty arrived to find him at the edge of her bed, about to take his clothes off, they grabbed him and dragged him outside. He fought back, saying she wanted him, saying she was the one who called to him from a window in the empty ward, and when they couldn't calm him down they tied him up and informed his unit. That was where the Commander found him—bound with rope in the medicine storeroom. Shalaby also didn't tell Ines or Um Mabrouk what happened next: that the Commander ordered Mahfouz to strip off his clothes and stand naked as the day he was born, while he blasted him with a hose and beat him with shoes and whips for disobeying orders.

He was supposed to have followed the orders he'd received before mobilizing toward the hospital, orders to stand on the mark the Commander had drawn on the ground, just like his fellow guards, and keep a safe distance from the sick ward. They told him not to abandon his post, under any circumstances, for any reason, but his lust for this woman had overpowered him. He was young, after all, and these things happen. Mahfouz was spotted later that day with his head hanging low, his bushy beard brushing against the hair on his chest. He groveled at his Commander's feet, saying again and again: "Do what you want with me, *ya basha*, I'll obey, sir, I swear." But Mahfouz was *mahzouz*—lucky—that it didn't go to trial and he wasn't summoned to the Gate. The woman wanted to protect her reputation, and in the end she didn't submit an official statement. Shalaby smiled, remembering that just a week after this incident Mahfouz survived that horrible accident, when their transport vehicle caught on fire and eleven of his fellow guards died. And then when the barracks collapsed with everyone inside, Mahfouz had emerged from the building without a scratch. But luck had betrayed him that final time during the Events, and now he lay like a stone at the bottom of the river.

Um Mabrouk lamented the loss of the young man and comforted Shalaby, patting him on the shoulder as tears filled her eyes. She had a sense that such a tragic situation was the perfect opportunity for her to tell her own story, about her daughter, and thereby win a bit of sympathy, but Ines seized her chance with an outburst, objecting to Mahfouz being called a martyr. She found herself opening her mouth without thinking again, and casting aside all virtues of silence, caution, and restraint. It was as if she'd left them all outside the classroom door and sauntered back into her Arabic lesson, where she'd always commanded attention.

Mahfouz had begun the attack and so he was to blame, said Ines. He'd killed someone first and paid a fair price. And what's more, the people who commanded him to kill should be punished too. Didn't people have enough to deal with every day, with their sorrows and troubles, and the anxiety of waiting, without people's lives being lost, too? And for what reason?

Um Mabrouk warily tried to silence her—you were never safe these days, not even from your own brother—and when she didn't succeed she edged away, said goodbye, and started to fiddle with her things. Ines continued her speech for a moment and then stopped, surprised with herself. For the first time in her life, she was speaking her mind in front of others, on a subject besides the lessons she taught her students. She was secretly pleased with what she'd said, and began to play it back to herself, word by word, carefully weighing up the meaning. Yes, she was confident in everything she'd said. Shalaby had provoked something in her, that ignorant fool who thought he was

76

the only one among them who understood anything. He spoke as if his cousin were a gallant knight at war with evil, and not a hapless soul plucked from his land against his will to serve in the security forces, when no one even knew what his unit did. Yet even so, Um Mabrouk was right. If anyone had heard her, or if Shalaby was well connected, he could report what she'd said to an inspector or the courts right away. She could be fired, not just reevaluated, and at that point not even the Certificate of True Citizenship she'd come for would be enough.

Shalaby turned on her like a lion, and would have slapped her across the face were he not so shocked. He could barely process everything he'd heard. No one had attacked Mahfouz's story before; the whole town remembered him proudly and considered him a hero for God and the Gate. People began to call Mahfouz's mother "Mother of the Hero," even "Mother of the Martyr," and she'd quickly adopted her new name. Shalaby spoke about Mahfouz every chance he got. "Oh, bless him," some would say; others would offer to help his family, and others shared his grief for his cousin. Still others praised Mahfouz's courage, bravery, and willingness for self-sacrifice, and some even cursed the men who had hounded him. But this woman standing before him understood nothing. Was she so ignorant that she didn't know the difference between a filthy criminal and an honorable man? Even if Mahfouz had made a little mistake here or there, he didn't endanger the country or its people like those rioters did. He'd sacrificed his life for it, and he was brave, maybe braver than all the other guards put together. He'd been a real man, while the man he'd killed— probably without even intending to—had been just a trouble- maker, a saboteur, out to frighten people and make their lives more difficult than they already were. That man had ground the country to a halt, he and others who shut down the streets while so many honorable citizens were just trying to earn their daily bread. All of Shalaby's cousins, and everyone he knew, had come home to the village and were now unemployed.

If he'd been in Mahfouz's shoes, he would've done what Mahfouz had done and more, and if Ines had been defending the nation in his place, she'd know how to obey orders. She would've learned that when you're given an order there's no discussion, no question, and barely enough time to carry it out—and even if there were time, the Commander wouldn't let you waste it with stupid questions. If he'd ever heard the things she said from one of his men, he would teach him a thing or two and then lock him up. If this woman had any honor, she would know that to obey your Commander was to obey God, and that insubordination was a sin greater than any mortal could bear and would lead to her own demise. But she was probably corrupt, morally and otherwise—no scruples, no religion, not even wearing a respectable headscarf; he could see a strand of hair hanging down beneath that pitiful scrap of fabric on her head. Yes, she was definitely one of the people the Commander had warned him about, just talking to her was dangerous, she might mess with his mind, try to brainwash him. If she wasn't one of them, why was she defending them and insulting his cousin, why was she happy that he was dead? She wouldn't agree that Mahfouz was a martyr, didn't think his family deserved to be compensated or that he was worth anything at all. It was possible that she had participated in the Disgraceful Events, too; he'd heard rumors that there were women saboteurs.

CELL SERVICE

Nagy discovered that Ehab knew much about life's mysteries from his work as a journalist and connections to people from all walks of life. Meanwhile, Ehab discovered that Nagy was a well-seasoned veteran of debates and clashes from both his university days and afterward, when he found a job. A long conversation unfurled between them as they told both the notorious and the unsung tales of their lives, exchanged thoughts on the latest developments in the district, and debated what they expected the Gate to do next. Of course it would open, they agreed, but when it did, it would become even more oppressive, and they wouldn't be rid of it anytime soon. Ehab was guardedly optimistic, while Nagy had long been burdened with an overwhelming sense of futility. In the course of their conversation, he brought up Yehya's ordeal and mentioned a few details, but not his friend's name or any information that might reveal why he was in the queue.

But Ehab began to act as though he had put two and two together. He started following Yehya around and checking up on him from time to time, even though his behavior aroused suspicion and Yehya tried to avoid him whenever he saw him coming. Eventually, Ehab convinced Nagy to reveal the rest of the story, thinking that he and Yehya might somehow need his help. From the moment when he understood the whole situation, Ehab refused to leave Nagy alone; he became single-mindedly focused on finding out when Amani was going to Zephyr Hospital. He knew how difficult her mission would be and smelled a story for the paper that was worth the risk. Obtaining any document from that place was like plucking a piece of meat from the mouth of a hungry lion, he said, and the odds of her failure were double those of success. His presence as a journalist could provide some backup and protection, he argued, and besides, he could be more tactful when he needed to be.

An evenly matched debate ensued, Ehab using his journalistic skills to convince Nagy, who resorted to the philosophical arguments in which he was well versed. Nagy didn't want to expose his friends or add a new level of complication, and he wasn't sure how Amani would react to Ehab. Nagy insisted that it was useless for Ehab or any journalist to go with her. He knew how capable Amani was (she could pluck the X-ray out of anyone's mouth—never mind a lion's) and knew she could do it herself. But despite Nagy's insistence, Ehab wouldn't stop pestering him until Nagy agreed to tell him the plan.

Um Mabrouk spread out her mat and began to sleep there most nights. Her son Mabrouk visited almost every day, and the queue delighted him with its potential for fun and games. He started to stop by after school, and soon he spent his weekends there. Away from their musty apartment, his health improved slightly; he gained weight, and his kidney attacks weren't so severe. One day he brought Um Mabrouk a message from his older sister, who rarely left the apartment these days, asking her mother to send her latest health report. Mabrouk said that she needed it immediately to attach to a job application for a position working at a Booth. Their expenses had doubled since Um Mabrouk had stopped working in the two additional homes, and instead divided her time between the Gate and the office where Amani worked.

From the sack she pulled a pile of papers, all in disarray, and stared at one page after another, but she couldn't find the report her daughter needed. Ehab was drawn to the commotion and offered to help. He crouched next to her and put the papers in order, by date: reports and patient certificates to one side, and examinations to the other. He was nearly finished and had just picked up the last few papers when he read the title on the first page and suddenly paused. His eyes widened, and the page trembled in his hand. On this yellow piece of paper, which didn't resemble the one before it, he'd found a short conversation. It had seemed familiar at first glance, though he didn't know where he'd seen or heard it. Then suddenly his memory breathed life into the words. It was a phone call he himself had made a couple of days earlier to a colleague at the newspaper. *"Saeed, things have gotten strange here. There are more and more people, the Gate is closed, and I'm hearing weird tales and stories. Let's meet next Saturday, I'll have written it all down by then."*

In the bottom left corner of the page, he read three words in thick red ink: *Important—Follow-up.* He turned the page and saw his own personal information, dead center, detailed and clear. There were more discussions and conversations in the following pages, but they were other people's, identified by names written on the back of every page.

Um Mabrouk noticed the sudden change that came over Ehab's face, and since she herself couldn't read, she asked if the report was really that bad. She wanted to know if her second daughter would die soon, just like her first, but he didn't answer her. He remained silent as a shade of red crept across his face and neck, and then his voice emerged, sticking in his throat, asking her where the papers had come from. He didn't understand anything she said; there were too many hospitals to count, and labs for analysis, and X-rays, and doctors in clinics and in centers, and health insurance; she told him there had been other papers but an official had taken them from her at the Booth right before she came to the queue, and then she made him swear to tell her the truth about her daughter's condition and why he was so alarmed.

He gave her the report she needed, and assured her that his reaction had nothing to do with her daughter; she'd just accidentally taken some other papers and he would return them to those to whom they belonged. Um Mabrouk clung to the pages and begged him not to lie to her, she'd endured so much and just wanted the truth, she told him, and her son began to cry. She wouldn't let him leave until he took the report, read it, and explained it to her in simple terms so she could understand. He promised to tell her the truth, and said she needed to finish her paperwork so she could do the surgery and save her daughter. His hands still trembling, he took the yellow pages, folded them carefully, and put them in his pocket. As he left, Um Mabrouk called after him with all the prayers she could remember. He headed to a place filled with scattered tree stumps and scraps of old cars, a place he would go whenever he wanted to write. He took out the papers and began to read them, patiently and deliberately, pausing over every word.

There were five pages in front of him. One was about him, another was about Ines, and the other pages concerned three people he didn't know, not their names, and not whether they were veterans of the queue or had never been there. He went back and watched Ines from afar. She was in her usual place. Um Mabrouk was rolling out her mat, Shalaby stood next to her, and a dish of *fuul* beans and a handful of pickles were sitting on a page of newsprint in front of them. Um Mabrouk offered Ehab some food as he approached, introducing him to Shalaby, but he shook his head, thanking her, and walked past them to Ines. He introduced himself, but she said she knew who he was—he was well known in the area, and she'd heard of him even though they'd never spoken.

He asked her if she could spare a few minutes so he could explain something important, out of earshot of the others in the queue. They took a few steps away from her mat, but she kept her eye on it, afraid that some opportunist might steal her place. Ehab took out the paper, told her to stay calm, and asked her to read it. Curious, she took the page. The conversation was long but she clamped her hand over her mouth when she read the first two lines, suddenly on the verge of tears.

"I'm really sorry, I'm sorry, I swear, I didn't mean anything by it, they're just words, I didn't mean to—"

He cut her off, saying there was no need to be sorry. He was in exactly the same position; there was a record of one of his phone calls on another page. Ines stopped crying and opened her mouth, but this time no sound came out.

"But I didn't talk to anyone on the phone today, or yesterday," she said suddenly, shocked. "I was talking to Shalaby, who was standing behind me." Holding the page tightly, she looked back at the others. "Shalaby, excuse me, do you have a minute?"

At first, Shalaby didn't understand what they were saying. Ines accused him of passing on what she'd said, but took it back when Ehab explained the situation. Shalaby hadn't listened to Ehab's phone calls and couldn't have passed them on, too, Ehab reasoned. Shalaby himself confirmed what Ines said—she hadn't spoken on the phone at all, nor left his sight since their conversation. He was telling the truth, he added, and this had nothing to do with how wrong she was about him or his cousin the martyr. Um Mabrouk interjected, too, swearing that Ines was a highly respected teacher. She had morals, her students learned a good deal from her, and she definitely hadn't said anything behind Shalaby's back.

THE SECOND DISGRACEFUL EVENTS

Hammoud locked and bolted the door to the coffee shop and shouted into his cell phone, which hadn't stopped ringing since he'd refused to serve the queue again. He wasn't coming back to work, he insisted, until the clashes around the coffee shop were dispersed and everything calmed down. The news spread through the queue within hours, and soon everyone knew that the Events had flared up again. It was the microbus drivers who began to keep people in the queue updated on the latest developments, although it wasn't easy for them to deliver news. According to new regulations, vehicles weren't allowed to drive alongside the queue anymore. The drivers had to leave their buses at the corner where a soldier stood, and then walk the rest of the way to the queue itself to pass on what they heard on their daily routes.

Most drivers continued to share updates that way, free of charge, for as long as the Events lasted, simply out of a sense of community. A deep-rooted friendship had grown between the drivers and the people waiting in the queue, and now it bore fruits of solidarity. No one expected the fighting to continue like this, and they wagered that life would soon return to how it had been before. Eventually, they told each other, the soldier would get used to them and allow microbuses to drive on the sidewalk again, as they'd been doing since the street had filled with people waiting in the queue. But their bets were lost in the blink of an eye. A big sheet-metal hut with two square windows appeared in the middle of the intersection one day, blocking the road, and not even the smallest cars could pass around it. The soldier was stationed inside it now, behind a sign with the phrase NO ENTRY FOR VEHICLES and the same signature, *Abbas.*

People who witnessed the Second Events described a battle that raged at the edge of the main square, but no one could tell exactly who the people involved were. There seemed to be different factions, but just like during the First Events, the combatants wore no uniforms and bore no symbols. No one involved would answer questions, and they ignored everyone else. Eyewitnesses disagreed over how many were injured and killed, and though the wails of ambulances were heard, no one saw anyone being transported away. Here and there, people noticed deep, wide puddles of blood, but only rarely did they see someone bleeding. A grizzled, stubble-chinned driver swore to a group of people in the queue that with his own eyes he'd seen a barefoot young man so wounded that his leg was about to fall off, his hand fiercely clasped around a clear plastic bag. Inside, the driver said he could make out small silver pellets, covered in a dark red liquid. The driver said that a plain-clothes officer had offered to buy the bag and everything in it, but the young man had grimly refused. A violent struggle had ensued, which ended with the officer stealing the bag and sprinting away with it before he could be stopped. The young man tried to chase after him, but his leg failed him, and he sat down on the ground and wept.

The Youth Channel presenter cried too, deeply affected by the events in the square. Her voice blared out of a radio inside a parked microbus, around which people from the queue had gathered. A well-known and respected psychologist was invited onto various news programs to explain and analyze the situation. He assured listeners that there was a very rational explanation for what was happening: the hot weather, which naturally leads to excitability, anger, and uncontrollable behavior. During one of these interviews, his explanation was interrupted by a news brief, which stated that officials were investigating the possibility of placing parasols near places of heavy traffic, to calm citizens' nerves and reduce their irritability.

No one knew what had started the Second Events, but on the first day of the fighting, Amani, who crossed the square nearly every day on her way to work, had seen people trying to sneak through the Restricted Zone. They were trying to reach a street that had long been closed off with iron barricades and was now a desolate stretch of land leading to the back of the Northern Building. No one was allowed there, and not even stray animals dared wander close. No signs or warnings were posted, but they wouldn't have been necessary. The street was surrounded by a colossal stone wall with no windows, impenetrable and impossible to scale, and which concealed the street and everything on it from passersby.

No one had been permitted to walk through the Restricted Zone for a long time, except for those carrying the Gate's violet ID card. Even so, people knew what was there, particularly the elderly, who'd known it before these changes. They said that the crimson Northern Building had been built over the street itself, or at least over half of it. The barricaded street led to a short tunnel, which passed under the Northern Building and came out the other side, somewhere near the Booth. One day, as she was about to leave the square, Amani heard things falling behind her, and the muffled sounds they made as their weight hit the ground, but she didn't turn around to see what they were. Suddenly, she sensed that the situation was more perilous than she had imagined, that things were about to explode, and she began to run to get away from the square, wanting to run away from everything, all of it.

The Events didn't deter Um Mabrouk from starting a little venture to help herself bear the cost of waiting in the queue, or at least offset the income she lost by no longer working in people's homes. Before, not a day would go by without one of the women she worked for giving her secondhand things for free; she came first in their eyes and was more deserving than strangers. She accepted them all, fixing things up into something she needed, but here in the queue, no one gave anything away. With her wide body and broad shoulders, she took up more space than most people in the queue, and she used this advantage as a starting point for her venture. She befriended a few drivers and asked them to bring her packages of tea, coffee, sugar, and powdered milk, which they delivered periodically and she paid for at the end of the week. She brought an old gas burner from home and bought cheap white plastic cups from a big chain store, which had opened several branches in her district overnight, and never seemed to close, not even during the Events.

When she returned from her work at Amani's office in the mornings, she would assume her position in front of the gas burner and provide drinks for the people around her. Her circle of customers quickly expanded. The coffee shop was closed and Hammoud had vanished, so she began to serve many people, veterans of the queue and newcomers alike. She considered

Ehab one of her most important customers, because every day he invited someone around for a cup of tea. The same went for Ines, who—since she was very methodical when it came to work—was used to drinking three cups of tea during the day: one during the first lesson, another during her break, and a last cup at night. They were soon joined by the man in the *galabeya*, who was constantly ordering new types of drinks, like anise tea, or cinnamon tea with ginger. Then Um Mabrouk added another service to the list. She let people use her phone at a discount price: they could call their loved ones for just half of what they would pay on their own phones or outside the queue. Before long, she was able to buy Mabrouk a new backpack for school, and then she gave him a bit of money to give to his sister. Her daughter still hadn't been able to find a job, even after she'd diligently attached her heath certificates and all other necessary supporting documents to her applications.

Um Mabrouk's venture was going better than she'd ever expected until life in the queue was disrupted by the clashes in the square. As the fighting peaked, the queue was stormed by a few of the "meddlesome riffraff," as Um Mabrouk had begun to call the protesters, a name soon adopted by others in the queue. The Riffraff cut part of the queue off and held hundreds of people captive behind barriers, which, she suspected, they had constructed out of the garbage and rubble that had piled up in the area. The people at the front of the queue finally glimpsed the Deterrence Force, which was meant to protect the Gate. The guards appeared, new shields in hand, and spread along the outer wall, but they didn't intervene.

When the people behind the barriers started to suspect that the Riffraff were trying to delay the opening of the Gate, they began to resent them—especially because there were rumors that the Gate's preparations had ended and it would soon open again. All sorts of evidence against the Riffraff began to appear, implicating them in a panoply of disgraceful acts. Accusations were broadcast all across the media, and serious allegations emerged that they were anti-Gate, followed by claims that they were trying divide and disperse the queue. Hearing this, the people behind the barriers rose up against the Riffraff, accusing them of behavior that was childish, frivolous, and irresponsible, and demanding that they leave immediately.

The Riffraff defended themselves fiercely, arguing that months had passed without the slightest change. People should unite and forget the Gate, they said, but they couldn't offer any convincing alternatives, so everyone in the queue—those behind the barriers and the rest—refused to give up hope. No one was ready to leave without receiving the resolution they had come for. Life in the queue had been relatively orderly and stable before the Riffraff's arrival; there were recognized rules and limits, which everyone accepted and everyone followed.

The one person who didn't join in this consensus was Nagy. He didn't tell anyone in the queue except Yehya what was on his mind. He wondered what made people so attached to their new lives of spinning in orbit around the queue, unable to venture beyond it. People hadn't been idiots before they came to the Gate with their paperwork. There were women and men, young and old people, professionals and the working class. No section of society was missing, even the poorest of the poor were there, not separated from the rich by any means. Everyone was on equal ground. But they all had the same look about them, the same lethargy. Now they were even all starting to think the same way.

He had expected there to be exceptions, that someone

among them would come out in support of the Riffraff, or even sympathize with their call to resist this absurd and ceaseless situation—but no one did. The queue was like a magnet. It drew people toward it, then held them captive as individuals and in their little groups, and it stripped them of everything, even the sense that their previous lives had been stolen from them. He, too, had been affected—he knew it in his heart. Otherwise, he would have still had his rebellious streak, and would have told everyone in the queue to advance, promising them that if everyone took just a single step, that single step alone could destroy the Gate's walls and shake off this stagnation. But the queue's magnet held him captive. Maybe he'd convinced himself that he was helping Yehya by staying in the queue, but the truth was he couldn't leave it; his body came and went, but his will was trapped here.

Everything ground to a halt. Daily life in the queue couldn't go on as normal, and it hurt people making a living there, including Um Mabrouk, who was forced to pack up her things and stop boiling water and rinsing out the cups she recycled, out of fear she would be attacked. Like many others, she'd received a threat from the Riffraff—though she wasn't sure she understood it completely—accusing her of helping to maintain the status quo, and even profiting from it.

Things soon reached a breaking point; there were negotiations and skirmishes, and the man in the *galabeya* set up prayers for those behind the barriers. People waiting in the queue began to offer compromises to the Riffraff: if the Gate didn't open within a month, they would sign a cessation of hostilities themselves, or would produce a written contract stipulating that everyone who had been in the queue for more than three months, including time spent away, would leave immediately. But none of these attempts to appease the Riffraff succeeded.

Then one day, they mysteriously withdrew. People simply woke up one morning and realized that the Riffraff were gone. They learned that the people behind the barriers had formed pacts and plans against the Riffraff, together with the microbus drivers, who had sensed impending danger when driving to and from the queue became forbidden. When the Riffraff realized that they would inevitably be driven away, they had rounded themselves up and departed in the night without a word.

The crisis had ended, but it left its mark on everyone in the queue, particularly on those who had received direct threats. It had been a waste of precious time for Um Mabrouk, yet more than that, it had restored her belief that misfortune followed her wherever she went. The drivers returned, supplying the queue with all the news they heard, but it was vague and infrequent. The warring parties had disappeared, but their effects lingered. The ambulance sirens could still be heard, but there were fewer and fewer of them, until finally peace prevailed, and then people learned just how many were injured and how badly.

Ehab stopped by nearly every day and Yehya began to check in with him, asking about the latest information he'd heard, but it wasn't of any use. The newspaper had no more news than anyone else; nothing—no statistics, no official messages—had been announced at all. The number of microbuses arriving at the corner dwindled, too. When none arrived for a few days, people realized that the gas stations were closed again and that all diesel fuel had been redirected to the arduous cleaning efforts. Scores of bulldozers arrived to clear the debris. They drove past the metal hut on the road to the queue, and some scraped it as they went by. But the soldier inside didn't reprimand them or even record their number plates. They worked in shifts for days on end, and then at different times at night for weeks, working without pause, lifting rocks and other debris, fallen tree trunks, and even trees still growing in the ground. Sometimes in the dark they picked up people sleeping, by mistake, but the people were always returned the following day, without having suffered significant harm.

A long time passed, and the Events had nearly faded into memory, when one morning the Gate broadcast a public message, declaring that the square was secure again and open to pedestrians. The Disgraceful Events were over, it said, never to return again, and it urged citizens not to be misled by what they had seen, no matter how confident they were in the accuracy of their vision. The broadcast also contained an important announcement: it was shutting down all radiology wards in hospitals, public clinics, and private clinics, confiscating all their equipment and taking it to Zephyr Hospital, which was a subsidiary of the Gate. The Gate had decided to embark on this path of comprehensive reform, the broadcast explained, in the interest of citizens' physical and psychological well-being. It had conducted follow-ups with patients across the nation, and determined that many of these devices gave false and inaccurate results and printed grainy or misleading images. These devices were being used with no consideration of medical or ethical principles, and any ward or clinic found to be in possession of such would be held accountable and punished accordingly. The message also called for anyone with an X-ray or medical test result of any kind to present it to the Booth immediately, so that it could be inspected and verified, and added that no fees would be collected for this complimentary service.

The announcement was delivered to the newspaper headquarters where Ehab worked, and he immediately called Nagy to tell him. Yehya headed straight for Um Mabrouk in shock, and dialed Tarek's number again and again. If the message were true, as everyone said, it meant he couldn't have an X-ray performed anywhere anymore, not even if he called in favors or tried to get one done under the table. When Tarek finally picked up, he didn't reveal anything on the phone, but he seemed more interested in Yehya than usual. He asked in detail about Yehya's movements, whether the pain was any less intense, if it was a stabbing pain or a throbbing pain. He asked how often Yehya urinated and what color it was, and he also asked about Amani. But Tarek's attention was useless to Yehya, who inferred just one thing: the head nurse still hadn't returned. She must have the X-rays, and Tarek was hiding the reason why she had left.

Um Mabrouk offered to waive the fee for his call and turned down Yehya's money out of sympathy for his injury. "The world is against you, you want me against you, too? *Ya ibni*, things are bad enough as it is." He left her, feeling like his head was about to explode. His memories rushed back to him and then faded away, leaving him in a tangle of conflicting emotions. He was filled with despair and a desire to hide away, but at the same time was infused with a yearning to survive, to start life anew and experience again every moment of sadness and joy and absurdity. He wasn't in the mood to argue with Um Mabrouk, but he also knew she didn't pay for the calls she made. Um Mabrouk had won a phone line and endless credit from Violet Telecom, just like so many others had.

Yehya had been on edge as he listened to Tarek's voice on the other end of the line. As soon as he ended the call he excused himself and left the queue, not heading anywhere in particular. He wandered around, taking in the whole scene from a distance. He knew he needed to see Tarek in private.

He returned a few hours later, cheerfully raising his fingers in a V when he saw Nagy. With a few niceties and a little flirting, he'd won Sabah over and learned that the head nurse had taken a long leave without pay. She'd turned in her notice, gathered her things, and gone to take care of some personal matters, staunchly refusing to discuss this sudden decision with anyone in the hospital. She'd been extremely secretive, concealing her decision until the day she left, and no one had been able to find out what had come over her, despite numerous attempts by her close friends and colleagues. Sabah also told him that she'd uncovered part of the secret herself. She'd learned that the hospital was considering hiring a new head nurse while the director thoroughly investigated the situation, which was this: a week ago, or perhaps more, the head nurse had joined the queue for the Gate.

MRS. ALFAT

Things soon returned to normal in the queue, and daily life picked up where it had left off. It was a charge led by Um Mabrouk, who got rid of her old cheap cups and bought nicer glass ones in celebration of the Riffraff's departure. She wiped her palms and the backs of her hands on her dress, and handed the man in the *galabeya* a cup of anise tea with two tea bags instead of just one, adding, "Lord grant you good health." He muttered a few words as he took the first sip, oblivious to her smile, but she persisted. "Don't you have a prayer, or something to say for heath and better days ahead, *ya Hag?*" she asked. He didn't indicate whether he had heard her, or if he had, whether he would respond, and didn't lift his gaze from the cup. Her smile faltered and she backed off, embarrassed, saying, "Ah, maybe you didn't hear me . . . don't worry, take your time." He finished the last drop of anise tea, quickly glanced at her from the corner of his eye, and wiped his beard, staring at the simple setup around her. He took out his prayer beads and advised her, while thumbing one golden bead after another, to come to the lessons he gave at the front of the queue. Many of the righteous attended these weekly lessons, and some even came from beyond the queue. "Early next week," he said. "It would do you good to come, by the will of God Almighty."

Yehya began his search for the head nurse, but the queue was so vast that he couldn't easily scan the crowds for her.

He managed to search a small area, but it was just a drop in a bucket, while the queue was fathoms deep. He reasoned that he shouldn't limit his search to the end of the queue; he didn't think she would feel bound to the order of arrival and stay at the end. Besides, he knew that people often and easily switched places—he himself had skipped ahead of so many, and some people who arrived just a few weeks ago were now at the front, each thanks to his or her own methods or bargaining abilities. So he and Nagy agreed to divide the queue between them, setting forth from the same point and walking in opposite directions.

He had to stop and ask about her out loud every few feet; there was no other way to go about it. The only picture they had of her was the one in Nagy's mind—the last time he'd been to the hospital, Sabah had led him to the nurses' office and proudly pointed to a large frame filled with photographs of the doctors, nurses, and other hospital staff. She'd stepped close to the frame, stuck her finger on the neck of a middle-aged woman, and pointed her out: "Mrs. Alfat, the head nurse, and me standing next to her." The people in the queue weren't surprised by Yehya's question; they were used to people asking for one another, and to hearing helpful strangers pointing them in the right direction. Sometimes photographs were distributed, of adults and children alike, lost amid the crowds of the queue. It happened at mealtimes especially, when news and rumors dwindled, the general sense of apprehension faded, and everyone's attention turned to the person sharing food with them. Yehya met two nurses in his search, a technician and an eye doctor with her younger sister, but neither of them was Mrs. Alfat, and not a single person claimed to know her. Um Mabrouk volunteered to ask her customers, and instructed them to ask others in turn, explaining, "The head nurse is a real big shot, a distant relative of Yehya's."

Yehya and Nagy met back at their starting point having had no success. They were exhausted and convinced it would be impossible to keep searching without a thread to grasp at. At this rate, it would take nearly two months. They sat down to brainstorm a way to save time; they'd lost so much already. Nagy suggested that they ask for Ehab's help, but Yehya rejected the idea outright. He wanted to keep the matter within the tightest circle possible. But then he remembered that this irksome journalist, who had offered them his friendship from the start, by pestering him relentlessly, had already learned a great deal about him. It was information that Nagy had disclosed with the best of intentions, but it meant that his situation was no longer a secret. Ehab already knew everything. And despite Yehya's reservations, he couldn't deny that Ehab and his fellow journalists had proven methods, when it came to investigating, that might help lead them to their goal: the whereabouts of the head nurse.

There was no need to surrender to mistrust, he realized, nor was there need to be so stubborn. He trusted Nagy, and Nagy in turn trusted Ehab. Time was moving swiftly, and with it things changed quickly. They could no longer predict what tomorrow would bring, or what future events might throw the world into confusion again. Nagy ordered a cup of coffee and took it with him as he went to look for Ehab, while Yehya left the queue to use the toilet. He walked away slowly and painfully, pressing his palm against his thigh to support his weight. Sweat streamed down his face. It poured down between his stitched brows and spread over his nose and mouth, intensifying the scorching blaze that emanated from his skin, as if his head had become a small sun.

He had to stop every two or three steps to catch his breath and wipe his face, while other people kept moving all around him. Some of those who knew him offered to assist him, while others ignored him, accustomed as they now were to his aversion to chit-chat and unnecessary gossip, and the pauses they left in conversation. The woman with the short hair waved to him and he nodded at her, unable to lift his arm and wave back because of the pain. She ran to catch up and stopped in front of him, out of breath. She inquired after his health and offered him a clean cotton handkerchief, telling him to keep it. Then she asked about his thoughts on the forgotten bag, the catalyst to the conflict that had erupted between her and the man in the *galabeya* a while back. She wasn't sure where Yehya stood on the matter, she said, but she presumed he was on her side. From afar she'd noticed he'd developed a relationship with Ehab, the young journalist, the same one who'd intervened to rescue her from the situation she'd stumbled into, and then he'd become involved himself when he'd suggested how they could resolve the matter.

Yehya drew himself up taller at her question and stared at her. He'd completely forgotten about the entire affair. Recent developments and fresh troubles had accumulated around him and he could barely remember what had happened, apart from a few words and hazy images. But this woman seemed to have more than enough time for such things; she was clearly the type who went around sticking her nose in where it didn't belong, stirring up trouble or chasing after it, until she got what she wanted. He promised her he would discuss it with Ehab, and pointed to his place in the queue to show her where he could usually be found, his expression revealing nothing. His face remained composed as he walked away, but once he had crossed to the other side of the road and was finally alone, he let the pain thunder through him again as he emptied his bladder.

There were dark droplets of blood discoloring his underwear and the pain now gnawed at him harder than before. He'd hoped things wouldn't work out this way, turning from bad to worse. Tarek had explained so many possible outcomes during their first meeting: the most hopeful was that the bullet might surrender and settle somewhere safe, surrounded by the protective tissue that the body naturally forms around any foreign object that disturbs its natural integrity. Then all these elements would be become one: the bullet, tissue, and various unknown secretions forming a tranquil, untroublesome mass that would stay with him for the rest of his life. But it seemed the bullet had chosen another path, launching an incursion into his intestines, puncturing them and perhaps soon poisoning his blood.

He tried to dispel these unsettling thoughts and replaced them with more uplifting ones: Amani storming the hospital basement, striking down whoever opposed her and returning with the X-ray; Nagy tying Tarek up, then forcing him to perform the operation; an ornate wedding dais at the beginning of the queue, in front of the Gate, and a huge picture of him and Amani placed on the corner instead of the NO ENTRY sign; and finally, the two of them wrapped in a long embrace, lovingly entangled in each other, instead of this uncomfortable silence that had settled between them since his injury. He straightened himself up as much as the pain would allow and decided he would go to Ehab himself.

FOUR

Document No. 4

Patient History

The patient, Yehya Gad el-Rab Saeed, had an ordinary childhood and adolescence; he did not contract any illnesses of note, has not previously undergone surgery, and has no family history of disease. He has suffered episodes of anxiety and irritability, which, during his final years of university, led him to commit certain acts that may be described as rebellious. His supervisors recommended follow-up in this regard. These episodes returned several months after he had graduated and secured appropriate employment; the reason for their recurrence has not been determined, although it is likely they are responsible for certain aspects of his behavior, particularly recent behavior, as he was seen in the square on more than one occasion, when he had no reason to be there. All information relating to this matter has been recorded in his Personnel File.

Records were subsequently requested from his university and workplace, and examination of the observations recorded therein has established that the symptoms observed in the patient offer an incomplete picture, and thus prevent an accurate diagnosis. In addition to anxiety and irritability, other symptoms include an irrational belief that he can alter reality; a clear tendency to act in a socially unacceptable and unhealthy manner; and a sharp, unfriendly manner when interacting with others.

The first time Tarek read the document, he had to look up the symptoms to fully understand them, as they were well outside his area of expertise. He read it two or three times, and then it dawned on him that all the episodes mentioned in Document No. 4—episodes that, it was said, Yehya had succumbed to on more than one occasion—coincided with particular events. Some had occurred before the Gate appeared, and others shortly afterward. Tarek knew what had happened to Yehya during the first Disgraceful Events, and knew that Yehya had suffered episodes of pain so severe that they left him immobile, but Tarek hadn't noticed anything like these emotional episodes or other strange symptoms.

Tarek was interested only in matters relevant to his work as a surgeon: whether Yehya had previously undergone surgery, or had a disease that would prevent further operations. He found himself calling for Sabah and asking her if she had noticed any unusual behavior or symptoms in Yehya when he'd been at the hospital, or whether he'd behaved in any way that might have unsettled or bothered her, but she was quick to dismiss the suggestion and seemed surprised by the question.

He returned to the last paragraph, searching for a detail that might lead him to a possible diagnosis, but found nothing. He contemplated the three additional symptoms, trying them on for size himself. It wasn't hard: Tarek had certainly done a few things that his colleagues had deemed unacceptable, or at least unwise. Once, he had made an honest mistake while assisting on a difficult surgical operation, and they had called him crazy when he actually admitted it to his boss. As for a "belief that he can alter reality," it was true that when he was younger he'd been certain he could convince other doctors not to skip their shifts and keep to the schedule like he did . . . or, at least, as he had done until recent months. He realized that he was on the same path as Yehya, and that one of these days he might merit a document just like this one. He turned the page over, burying it among the other papers, and pushed the file to a far corner of his desk.

THE WAY TO THE COFFEE SHOP

Ehab shook Yehya's hand encouragingly, welcoming him into a relationship of friendship and solidarity, where he would be at Yehya's disposal. He told Yehya that he was ready to help him any way he could, with anything and at any time. Whether he was in the queue or at the newspaper headquarters, all Yehya had to do was call him. He gave him his phone number and left him with Nagy; he didn't want to waste time talking when he was sure he could find this Mrs. Alfat, wherever she was. If Yehya was ready to go public with his story, which was sure to spark an uproar, he would be by far the most important person Ehab had met in the queue; he and his bullet were pieces of solid evidence that hadn't yet been covered up. If Yehya was able to get his permit, it would set a significant precedent; the Gate had never issued anything like it before. But if he failed, he would pay with his life, and no bargaining or compromises would save him. Ehab meant it: he was ready to do anything to help Yehya stay strong until the Gate opened. He and Nagy could take care of anything Yehya couldn't do himself—any difficult tasks that could cause Yehya's health to take a turn for the worse. There was no question that the two of them were faster than he was, but he refused to stop coming and going. He kept fighting against it all, even though it was exhausting his ailing body and he desperately needed to rest. Ehab had been interested in Yehya since he first laid eyes on him and his perpetual frown. It didn't seem to match Yehya's admirable fighting spirit, but from the time they'd first met in the queue, Ehab didn't remember ever having seen Yehya smile.

A few days after the Gate released its announcement, Amani called Nagy from the office. She'd been debating what to do, and trying in vain to reach Yehya, and she was so anxious by the time she phoned Nagy that she didn't even wait for an answer when she asked how he was, and leapt right into her next question:

"Did you hear the message?"

"I heard it."

"What about Yehya?"

"Yehya heard it, too. We're looking for the head nurse."

"I think we really screwed up. We got off to a late start; Yehya should've requested the X-ray sooner."

"We would have run into the same problems either way. That or other problems. Now's not the time for blame, Amani."

"*Tayyeb*, all right. Listen, I took two days off work, and I'm going to Zephyr Hospital tomorrow or the day after."

"Call me before you go, Amani, please . . . or better still, let's meet up beforehand. We can meet you anywhere near the queue."

"Fine. Tomorrow at three at the restaurant across from the coffee shop?"

"We'll see you there."

"Tell Yehya I say hi. And can you convince him to get a new cell phone? I can't stand not knowing how to get hold of him."

Yehya, meanwhile, was rather pleased to be working with Ehab, who wasn't nearly as nosy as he'd feared. Perhaps he'd been mistaken about him; maybe he'd been overly annoyed by his loud personality, or maybe he'd just lost patience with

Ehab's constant buzzing beside him, the pecking that threatened to bore holes straight through him. Yehya wasn't sure when Ehab would be back, but he wasn't worried. A strange mood had taken hold of him recently: the significance of life's minutiae waned and dwindled before his eyes, and suddenly everything seemed inconsequential.

Standing there in the queue, he toyed with the possibility of freedom; he wanted, even if only in the smallest way, to cast off what he was used to doing so mechanically and to break the tedium of these countless weeks of waiting. He marked his place on the ground, told people nearby that he was leaving, as was customary in the queue, and then decided that for the rest of the day he would no longer do what was expected of him. He woke Nagy up from his nap and told him he wanted to wander through the downtown area of the city for a while. Nagy stood up, wiped his face with his shirtsleeve, passed his fingers through his hair, and looked ready for action. He hadn't expected Yehya to leave the queue again, not after their last and only excursion, to see Tarek, which had ended in disappointment. They walked side by side, occasionally linking arms, and without a word they headed toward the old coffee shop. It was where they'd often met up in their student days, and they hadn't been there for years, although they'd heard recent reports that it was almost in ruins after surviving numerous attacks.

A warm breeze blew on their faces from the direction of the coffee shop, but it carried the pungent gas that still lingered in the streets, making their noses run and their eyes sting. The world looked like it had the day they went to see Amani: the ground was crushed, and deep fissures ran through the asphalt, as if creating new streets. Their eyes fell on a scattering of strange, large, multicolored munitions. They didn't look like anything Yehya and Nagy had ever seen before, and offered no trace of where they might have been manufactured.

There were empty tear-gas canisters strewn in the stretches between the munitions all the way to the coffee shop. Nothing they remembered was as it had been, except for the beggar lady, whom they knew well from their university days. As they drew closer, they caught sight of her sitting in her usual place under the violet sign, but her things, which had long been the same, were slightly altered. A gold medallion on a dark-blue ribbon now hung in front of her, next to an old kerosene stove, a cup of tea, and her usual packets of tissues for sale.

In Nagy's eyes, she'd earned that medallion as a badge of honor for refusing to leave her place during the times when the street had been filled with tear gas. She'd sat cross-legged in her usual place, not moving an inch, not trying to hide, a helmet on her head, a black gas mask hung around her neck, while everyone else was running all around her. She'd reached the pinnacle of valor, her hand always extended in front of her, clearly signaling she was begging for change. After all, one must not stop working, no matter what the circumstances were. Yes, he thought, clearly she'd realized that the economy was lifeblood itself! That the wheel of production and construction must not stop spinning, not even for a moment, not even in the darkest of times. He smiled cynically at his own thoughts. If he hadn't made that valiant decision—a valiant stupidity, he admitted at times—to resign from his position at the university, where students often missed classes and didn't ask much of the lecturers, he would have presented her to his advanced students. He would have asked them to conduct a study on the philosophy of time, space, and physical existence, and then write a short paper inspired by her: the Lady with the Mask.

THE GATE'S ANNOUNCEMENT

For as long as they could remember, the television had been sitting on a thick wooden shelf high up on a wall in the coffee shop, stuck on one channel. It couldn't get any other signal, the boy who worked there often announced. Or maybe it was Hammoud who constantly claimed that the thing was broken, just stuck on the same channel, and never gave customers the chance to ask to change it. With practiced care, Yehya slowly bent his right knee, leaned his torso to the right, too, and then lowered one side of his skinny bottom onto the edge of the wooden chair. He let the pain swell to its full magnitude for a moment, until he knew he could bear it without groaning or crying out, and then slid his whole rear end onto the rough-edged wooden seat, stretching his left leg out a bit. From their table on the sidewalk in front of the coffee shop, they could see that the damage hadn't been serious. Some glass cups had cracked, a few chairs had lost a leg or two, and an antique painting had fallen from the wall where it had hung. Nagy poked his head inside the coffee shop but didn't see Hammoud, just a few customers staring at the television while the backgammon sets and domino pieces sat untouched. He turned his gaze toward the television, watching it carefully, and then placed a cautionary hand on Yehya's shoulder. The Gate rose up on the screen in its full splendor as the announcer's voice proclaimed with zealous delight:

"O beloved fellow citizens, in order to fully cater to your needs, the Gate shall soon extend its exceptional services to you every day of the week, from seven in the morning until four in the afternoon each day. Please complete your paperwork before reserving a place and deliver it to the Booth, making sure to keep the receipt signed by the official as proof of validity. For applicants for Certificates of True Citizenship, your application must be accompanied by an official letter notarized by your place of work or study, stating the purpose of your request, the party to which the Certificate shall be sent, as well as confirmation of their eligibility to receive it. Do not hesitate to inquire about the following numbers . . ."

The announcement lasted seven whole minutes, and Nagy watched them tick by on his watch one by one. Afterward, a phrase no one in the coffee shop had seen before appeared on the screen, as though it were an addendum, unconnected to the audio recording. *With regards from Former Major General Zaky Abd el-Aal Hamed, President of the Northern Building.*

Nagy looked away and smiled. Despite how often the Gate released these promising updates, it still had never reopened, and nothing ever really changed. All it provided was hope for people to cling to and a reason to stay in the queue. The Gate had started producing these announcements shortly after it appeared and initially aired them on several different channels. Before long, a special channel was created to broadcast all Gate-related news, then related fatwas as well, and recorded messages aimed at citizens, too. After that, the special channel began to broadcast new laws and decrees as the Gate issued them, one after the next, and forbade other channels from showing them. Then it decided to list the names of people whose applications and permits would be approved when the Gate opened, listing them on-screen at the end of every week.

This attracted a huge viewership; people delighted in discovering who among them had been lucky and who had been rejected. Later, the Gate issued a decree that forbade other channels from screening any announcements other than its own and forced them to air its broadcasts instead. Its messages had become increasingly aggressive and intense, particularly after the Disgraceful Events, and it made the other channels replay them all. Some networks complied, but others refused and instead shut down their channels and offices. The Gate didn't regulate radio stations the same way, though. It simply made sure it held sway over employees at the stations, and recruited loyal citizens, men and women alike, to call in to the programs while posing as unbiased listeners.

Hammoud appeared about half an hour later carrying a tray of drinks, and stopped short in front of them, understandably surprised. Seeing them outside the queue, right here under his nose, was the last thing he'd expected. Nagy reproached him for disappearing so suddenly and abandoning the residents of the queue without a hint or warning, but Hammoud said the situation had become so dangerous that he had no choice but to serve the construction workers instead. He was sorry, he said, but he was also fed up with the way things were going, especially with Um Mabrouk, who'd overstepped her bounds.

"What does she know about tea and coffee?" He began to shout. "Shouldn't she just stand in the queue like everyone else? Why's she cutting into our business?"

He accused the two of them of collaborating with her to hatch a plot against him and the coffee shop's owner; it wasn't right that they'd lost so many regular customers to Um Mabrouk, and so quickly, too. People could have waited until life returned to normal, things in the neighborhood calmed down, and the coffee shop opened its doors again, but no—no one had said a word, and no one thought to dissuade Um Mabrouk. Most of them had encouraged her to stay in business and even to expand. Hammoud carried on, growing so furious that he was ready to start an actual fight or even throw them out, but thanks to Yehya's patience they rode out his anger and then countered his rant, turning the tables on him with playful banter. Wasn't there a well-known brand of tea, Nagy said, whose taste mysteriously changed when it was in Hammoud's hands? And which they had discovered—purely by chance, of course—was cut with some kind of black powder: watered down, just like the rest of his drinks were? Winking at each other, they told him that that was the real reason they supported Um Mabrouk, and Hammoud gave in. He laughed without commenting on or denying their accusations, and then went to get their drinks: two cups of coffee with sugar, in proper glasses instead of the usual cheap cups.

A man wearing a traditional striped *galabeya* walked past them with a large stack of newspapers hanging from a wide leather band wrapped around his middle. He looked like an old-fashioned street peddler, but didn't announce his wares as the old hawkers once did, and he walked by dull-wittedly, as if he had run out of exciting headlines that might attract potential business. Nagy called out to the man, who seemed disinterested in the possibility of customers, and he ploddingly turned around and reluctantly returned to where the two of them were sitting. Yehya asked him about a certain economics magazine and Nagy requested one of every newspaper and magazine the man was carrying, but the man drearily apologized: the only paper he was selling was *The Truth*.

Nagy bought a copy and tossed it down on the table, which was spotted with small puddles of water. The paper's edges began to soak it up, softening, becoming translucent, and revealing the pages beneath. Hammoud arrived with their coffee and Nagy pushed the paper aside to make room for the cups. A mischievous half-smile formed on Hammoud's lips when he saw the wet paper, the pages warped and stuck together. The front-page headline read "NEW AMENDMENTS TO LAWS AND DECREES" and was followed by a few brief sentences and a note that the amended laws could be found inside. Nagy's eyes fell on a familiar phrase, dead-center on the page: *Authorization for the Removal of Bullets*. Article 4 (A) was one of the amended articles. The text of the article had not been changed, but now there was an additional paragraph. Nagy shifted in his seat, reading the front page warily, but said nothing. He didn't want to spoil the relatively good mood that had come over Yehya, so he folded the newspaper, set it aside on a chair, and clapped for Hammoud, calling out, "Another coffee, and tea with mint."

Not an hour after Yehya and Nagy left the coffee shop, Hammoud heard the announcer's voice return on the television, more solemn and stern this time. The announcer himself appeared, wearing a sleek jacket and gray tie with diagonal stripes, his face filled with gravitas. At the end of his segment, he added that he'd just received several important decrees issued by the Gate, and listed them in succession. He devoted special attention to the revision of Article 4 (A), saying that it had been amended in accordance with a new spirit in government emphasizing sound moral principles and surveillance of

113

citizens' consciences. He also added that it had been altered as a direct response to developments in the country, and was in effect immediately.

"*Permits authorizing the removal of bullets shall not be granted, except to those who prove beyond doubt, and with irrefutable evidence, their full commitment to sound morals and comportment, and to those who are issued an official certificate confirming that they are a righteous citizen, or, at least, a true citizen. Certificates of True Citizenship that do not bear a signature from the Booth and the seal of the Gate shall not be recognized under any circumstances.*"

The voice rattled on with rationale and regulations before presenting the rest of the news, none of which contained anything new, and Hammoud wiped down the tables and dried them with a couple of pages he'd ripped from the newspaper that Nagy and Yehya had left behind. He raised the volume on the television a little and adjusted the image. Along with the money he earned from waiting tables at the coffee shop, he could count on keeping this channel on for as long as possible.

As soon as they left the coffee shop, Nagy went to Ehab to discuss the latest amendment, without telling Yehya, who didn't need to be burdened with even more trouble. His usual air of despondency and distress had lifted in the last couple of days, and there was no need to bring it back. There was now yet another document to add to the growing stack of papers he needed to qualify for a permit; the road ahead grew longer, more difficult, and ever more complicated. As Yehya walked up to them, they fell silent.

"Alfat still hasn't appeared, Ehab?"

"Don't worry, I haven't forgotten about it . . . If she's in the queue, I'll find her. I've asked a bunch of people I know to help look."

Yehya nodded and then took a drab, square piece of paper that looked like a government receipt out of his pocket. The Booth had accepted his ID card, he said, the one from work, even though it had expired. The official had photocopied it twice and told him there was just one more step: a personal interview at the Gate. If he passed this and was granted a Certificate of True Citizenship, it would automatically be added to his file there, along with the rest of his papers and documents. Then, when the Gate opened, they would consider his application for the permit to extract the bullet.

Nagy was stunned and Ehab laughed, impressed—Yehya did not disappoint. Despite adversity, Ehab thought, he always moved in the right direction, not hesitating, not waiting for help or even advice from those around him. He knew about the amendment, decided to take action, and did it himself, all while Ehab and Nagy were still discussing what to do. He was a marvel. If you'd seen him two days ago, walking doubled over, ashen-faced and miserable, you would have thought he had given up completely, surrendered like so many others had done. Other people had weakened when faced with fear and pain, or submitted to the flood of pressure and promises from above, clinging to a desire to survive their predicament. Others agreed to undergo surgery at Zephyr Hospital and somehow emerged as they'd been before the Disgraceful Events. They didn't have a mark on their bodies, no signs of bullets or shrapnel, and the operations left almost no trace. But Yehya wasn't like them. He was a different kind of man, steadfast and stubborn, and must have realized that day in Zephyr Hospital how important his injury was: he was carrying a government bullet inside his body. He possessed tangible evidence of what had really happened during the Disgraceful Events, and was perhaps the only person still alive who was willing to prove what the authorities had done.

But Ehab brushed these thoughts aside and quickly interjected before either of the others could speak.

"It's good what you did, Yehya . . . You've got to act fast in times like these."

"Now we just need the Gate to open. Everything else depends on that."

"Nagy, have you called Amani yet?" Ehab asked. "I'm determined to be with her when she goes to the hospital."

"She called, and Yehya and I said we'd meet her tomorrow afternoon at the restaurant by the coffee shop."

"Great. Make sure she doesn't forget to tell me when she's going to the hospital, so I can be ready."

Ehab left them to finish his rounds and they sat down together, hoping for some brief respite before returning to their place. The queue forked around here and extended ever farther, and no one cared to speculate how long or vast it was anymore. Whole families came to visit their relatives waiting there, children played on the sidewalk and hurled their leftover food at the soldier sitting in his metal box. Microbuses had begun to arrive regularly again, and the gas stations had opened after the cleansing operations finished. The insects, though, hadn't disappeared.

When they returned to their place, they found the young man who'd carried the old Southern woman away. He said his mother was well, that she was resting at home, and with the utmost courtesy asked if he could take her place in the queue, peering over at the place she'd vacated. Ines immediately said yes and let him stand in front of her, and as soon as he unpacked and settled in, she leaned over and asked how sick the old lady was, and why she'd fainted, but the young man wasn't as forthcoming as Shalaby. She asked him politely, but he responded with just a few terse words, so Ines repeated her questions several times, hoping—in vain—for something that would satisfy her curiosity. The man in the *galabeya* began to make frequent visits to the area, too, and he stood around without any apparent reason, announcing how displeased he was with the disgraceful mingling between men and women. Soon he turned his attention to Ines, telling her to conduct herself with modesty, not to lean forward or bend over, and to pray, so that God would answer her prayers and send her what she needed from the Gate.

Ehab ran into the woman with the short hair during an interview he was doing near Um Mabrouk. He greeted her warmly and, remembering their first meeting, told her lightheartedly that the lost bag was likely still lost—after everyone had agreed to his idea, the man in the *galabeya* had kept it in the end. He followed this with a hearty laugh, expecting her to join in, but displeasure flickered across her face. She was not at all amused; she took the matter seriously and felt that he'd failed her. She'd put her faith in him and he wasn't acting like a real journalist should, with principles and skills. The crowd swelled around them, with people eating and drinking on one side and those waiting to be helped by Um Mabrouk on another, and the woman with the short hair gave up on the discussion. She shook her head in frustration and then glanced at her watch, as if in excuse, and returned to her place in the queue with the little radio she always carried.

Ehab spent two nights outside the queue and returned early the third morning with a copy of the newspaper he wrote for, which had published an important investigative piece he had written on additions to and deletions from the amended laws and decrees. He'd conducted interviews with people who were concerned with the issue, and explained in his article that despite how carefully the amended clauses must have been considered, there were a few things people objected to. He cited clause 4 (A) as an example, writing that the amendment had sparked considerable controversy, particularly from groups defending people's rights. They pointed out how complex the law was—or "intricate," as they put it—and respectfully suggested that it might be difficult for people to comply.

For example, some of those who had bullets lodged in their bodies were critically injured and incapable of submitting an application, waiting for their cases to be evaluated and substantiated, and then completing the paperwork for surgery permits.

Other groups condemned both the original text and the amendment to clause 4 (A). Their critique seemed objective and fair: Zephyr Hospital—the sole hospital exempt from the permit requirement—had only so many beds. If the Disgraceful Events flared up again, or other unrest broke out, it might not be able to accommodate all the injured. Some people might be forced to seek treatment in unregistered and unsafe hospitals, which would unleash a new wave of problems.

At the end of his article, Ehab cited an anonymous proposal

that had been sent to the newspaper. It asked the Gate to open up other authorized branches in additional selected hospitals. With more hospitals operating under the Gate, surgery would become easier and more affordable. This move would also put a stop to all the wild rumors that the government was somehow to blame for the injuries, when all it sought to do was help the injured and, of course, protect the rights of its citizens.

Little by little, Um Mabrouk discovered that aside from her snacks, drinks, and cell phone, which at times drew several sub-queues of customers at once, the woman with the short hair attracted even more people just by being there. She watched her carefully, and soon realized that the throngs of people flocking to her stall and seating area had nothing to do with the woman herself but with her radio. Um Mabrouk reasoned that it created an inviting and lively atmosphere, which encouraged people to stay longer and order more drinks and sometimes roasted sweet potatoes and packets of cookies. Based on these observations, she began to invite the woman over to her stall every time she walked by. She was as friendly as could be and used every trick in the book to keep her there, until finally she made a generous offer that the woman agreed to. Um Mabrouk said she would give her free tea for as long as she stayed there, as long as the radio station played what people wanted to hear, not what she herself preferred.

THE BOYCOTT CAMPAIGN

As expected, Violet Telecom's promotion was a huge success in the queue, and there seemed no limit to the number of free phones and contracts the company was willing to give away. But it suddenly came under close scrutiny when people made an unnerving discovery.

Their phones had begun to record their conversations and were transmitting them to a receiving device in the Booth. Somehow both phone calls and discussions happening around the phone were all being recorded—even when they weren't actually making a call, and even when their phones were turned off. Ehab confirmed it: he'd been leaked top-secret information that the official in the Booth attached to the Gate was meant to review conversations and determine which of them indicated a degree of threat. He sent his evaluations directly to the basement of the Northern Building, where the conversations underwent a careful process of inspection and classification. These were added to the individual phone owner's file, and in some cases, immediate actions were taken. Ehab also explained to people in the queue that when everyone's phones had stopped working a couple of weeks ago, it had been a trial period. The company had been experimenting with the data-collection feature, and caused the outage in order to activate it on all of its customers' phones, but the feature had worked only briefly. Instead, with the assistance of specialists, the company had hand-selected the most important conversations. It culled the most enigmatic and suspicious ones, those related to the Gate's security, and put those people under constant surveillance. Then, to bring them into the network, it offered some of them free phone lines.

Ines had solid evidence to back up everything that Ehab had reported. Over afternoon tea, she confided in the woman with the short hair that she'd been shaken to discover she was under surveillance herself. She told the woman about her conversation with Shalaby, in which every syllable and every word had been recorded. Um Mabrouk confirmed the incident. Ehab produced the papers he'd kept, which included the whole conversation and many others. They had been stamped by the Booth and officially approved by the official, and he offered to show them to anyone who wanted to see them. With this discovery, and similar evidence that began to follow it, people stopped using phones, both their own and Um Mabrouk's, except on rare occasions, and a wide-reaching boycott campaign gathered momentum. When Um Mabrouk announced that she was joining the campaign, her son removed the battery from her phone and took it back home. She rather liked the boycott, and was a staunch supporter. She was excited to join Ehab and his friends, and told her customers the part of the story that she herself was involved in, embellishing it with just a few tantalizing details.

People gradually discovered that the surveillance feature had spread beyond the queue and into other districts. No one knew whether it affected everyone, or just the free phone lines, or only those people whose conversations had been sent to the basement. Despite the public outcry, Violet Telecom continued to give out free phones, and a few days later published an advertisement in *The Truth* promising its customers a superior new service, with details to be announced in an upcoming offer. The company also warned citizens against believing false information spread by its less fortunate competitors, information that only aimed to tarnish its reputation and to deprive vast segments of the population—particularly the poor—from its free services. Meanwhile, rumors spread that some people whose conversations had been recorded had disappeared; they'd been summoned to the basement and never returned. These rumors left a visceral tension in their wake; people in the queue exchanged names of the disappeared and the dates they'd vanished, distributing flyers with their pictures and pleas to return them unharmed. Even though no one from the queue was missing, Ines was so overwhelmed by the situation that her support for the boycott began to wane, even though she'd been one of its first champions. She grew increasingly timid and withdrawn, and stopped drinking tea with Um Mabrouk.

But the woman with the short hair urged the boycott campaign onward, undaunted by the obstacles ahead. The vast majority of the queue joined her, those who were particularly keen to help rally others from farther afield, and she even considered extending an invitation to the outlying districts. Yet despite the campaign's growth, nothing in the papers seemed to indicate that Violet Telecom had been affected in the least. Several papers published full-page advertisements featuring its name and bright violet logo. Then an article appeared in *The Truth*, so large it took up nearly half the front page, which said that Mr. Zaky Abd el-Aal Hamed, CEO, was delighted to announce that Violet Telecom now served more than thirty percent of the population. This meant that it was now the most widely used phone company in the country, and by a significant margin; the next most popular company served no more than five percent.

Yet while no newspapers or magazines covered the Violet Telecom boycott, their pages were filled with enthusiasm for other boycotts—all led by something called the Fatwa and Rationalizations Committee. The first boycott was against a candy factory that owned a well-known chain of stores in several districts. The Committee had discovered that this factory was producing candy made of sugar swirls, in which—in a certain light—one could make out the word "God." The Committee released a statement calling upon people to boycott the factory, since allowing the name of God to be eaten and digested was the ultimate denigration of religion's place in society and thus warranted a country-wide campaign.

Shalaby joined this boycott, too, after he recognized the factory's name from some candy he'd brought along with a few other snacks from a small shop in his hometown. Pleading for God's forgiveness and protection, he immediately destroyed the candy and burned the wrapper, as people around him cried out in praise of God's greatness and commended his victory over the factory owner. The man in the *galabeya* had joined the boycott before him, and the two of them were joined by Um Mabrouk (who asked Abbas to write "Hope Factory Products Not Sold Here" on a cardboard sign, which she then put between two stones in front of the cookies), and the three of them were joined by Mrs. Alfat, who had finally appeared at the front of the queue.

Yehya insisted on crossing the vast distance to Mrs. Alfat himself. When he heard the news, Nagy tried to go in his place, but Yehya wouldn't let him, that he would meet with her himself, and he set off as soon as they knew it was definitely her. Ehab described her as a short woman in her fifties, of medium build, and with broad shoulders. She was wearing a thin veil, only one layer of fabric, and no makeup except a thick line of kohl around her eyes. He also said that she was wearing wide-legged trousers, a long gray jacket that came down to her knees, and, unlike most other women, sneakers.

Yehya had no trouble recognizing her. He found her standing at the front of the queue already, not taking part in any of the conversations around her but clearly listening attentively to all that was said. She seemed on edge, uneasy with the general atmosphere. Yehya stood there for a few minutes watching her from afar, and to him she seemed stern, despite how calm and beautiful she looked. What would compel someone like her to leave such a prominent position? What had prompted her to abandon her workplace and home to stand in the queue just like him? So many thoughts and possible explanations rushed through his mind, but none of them made sense. He tried to guess how she might respond to his surprise visit, but soon tired of his useless speculations and felt silly waiting there so aimlessly, so he drew a deep breath, let it echo in his injured side, and headed toward her.

"Good afternoon."

"Hello . . . can I help you?"

"My name is Yehya Gad el-Rab Saeed. I was a patient at the hospital you worked at."

"Ah, pleasure to meet you. Is there something I can do for you?"

"Well, Dr. Tarek wanted to get ahold of the X-ray he performed on me at the hospital, but you were on vacation, so—"

"An X-ray of what, exactly?" she asked, cutting him off.

"An X-ray of my pelvis."

"And when was this?"

"June eighteenth."

Yehya would have preferred not to have to mention anything that might put her on guard, and instead to have left it up to her memory.

"The day of the Disgraceful Events," she said sharply. "Sir, I didn't receive any paperwork or X-rays that day—not yours, nor of anyone else who was injured, nothing. Even the people who died were then transferred to Zephyr Hospital. I'm quite certain you know that."

Yehya was surprised by her cutting response, which didn't leave him much room to respond.

"But Dr. Tarek took an X-ray of me, ma'am, I saw it myself, and just the other day he told me you had it."

"That's simply not true. I would advise you to meet with him again."

He thanked her and left. He didn't have the energy to argue or make her repeat herself, or even question her response; it was as if he'd known what she would say from the start. The door Tarek had opened for him had just been slammed in his face.

Amani, Yehya, and Nagy were forced to put off their meeting for several days, as the events unfolding around them didn't leave time for much else. Nagy had been busy going over the conversations he'd had lately, reviewing what he had said and how involved he had been in them, so that he wouldn't be caught off-guard if something happened. Finally, they all made time to have lunch at a restaurant across from the coffee shop.

Amani sat beside a large glass window, gazing down from the second floor onto the narrow street below, which seemed to have been cleaned of all shrapnel and debris recently. The restaurant hadn't changed much since the last time she was here: the same scent of cheap detergent, the dark-green chairs, the small tiles that never reclaimed their true whiteness, the clay pots with edges eroding from how often the plants were watered; even the number of customers seemed the same. Amani had chosen her usual table. Twice she waved away the waiter, waiting for Nagy and Yehya, who were running late, and passed the time by watching people walking briskly below, imagining the two of them meandering along as usual.

It took a long time for Yehya to walk up the stairs, gripping the handrails for support and leaning his weight on Nagy's shoulder. He never imagined that he would struggle up a flight of stairs like this, especially while still young. The pain peaked on the last step, and he stood paralyzed for a moment. Then finally he let go of Nagy and the railing and dropped his hands to his sides. He smiled, struggling to breathe normally, and headed to where he knew Amani would be sitting. He stood behind her chair and placed his hands on her shoulders, burying his lips in her hair for a long kiss. The waiter, having run out of patience, was back at their table for the third time as soon as they took their seats. Amani was about to tell him off, but Nagy, who had noticed the telltale way she was pursing her lips, that ominous sign that meant she was ready for a fight, intervened. He quickly ordered some eggplant, *fuul* beans, and fried eggs, while Yehya sat holding Amani's hand and catching his breath.

Their conversation was dominated by recent developments; Yehya and Nagy had collected a bounty of intriguing news from around the queue, and took turns telling the stories. The woman with the short hair had earned even more animosity from the man in the *galabeya*; he disapproved of her stances on many issues, and it riled him so much that he wanted to banish her from the whole district. Ines had matter-of-factly declared that she wasn't convinced by the Violet Telecom boycott without offering a reason, though she was often seen crying now that the rumors of the disappeared had grown more grave.

The man in the *galabeya* had begun to appear beside her at all hours, and people saw him talking to her at length, sometimes even shouting. Sometimes she cried harder when he was around, and other times her tears abated, but no one heard exactly what he said.

Amani had no news from the office, just that Um Mabrouk was often absent. Nagy explained that even though she was doing good business in the queue, he imagined she would return to honor her responsibilities at the office—particularly given the current situation. She had recently gotten rid of her phone, and her revenue had dropped sharply.

They rapidly exchanged news, falling silent for just a moment here or there and then picking up the conversation again, while the waiter punished them for their delay in ordering by delaying their food in turn.

Yehya had avoided revealing what had happened between him and Mrs. Alfat, but there was no way to avoid it when the other two asked him straight out if he was hiding something. Amani didn't believe the head nurse, and called her a snake, while Nagy accused Tarek of lying. Yehya didn't side with either of them, but flat-out refused the suggestion that they go back and face Tarek in the hospital again. If Alfat or Tarek had any intention of giving him the X-ray, they would've done so, but they both denied they had it, and Yehya had no way to prove it had ever even existed. Confronting them about its disappearance might just make things worse. The levity with which they had begun the afternoon dissipated, and each of them turned to the plates of food that had arrived, isolated in their individual thoughts.

After slowly finishing her food, Amani solemnly announced that she'd go to Zephyr Hospital early the next morning. Yehya tried to dissuade her, but she pointedly ended the discussion. She had delayed it long enough, she said, and she didn't need anyone to discourage her now. She was even more worried now that Yehya had confirmed that the X-ray was lost, and that was enough to convince her that she had to go. She could barely keep herself in her chair; she rocked back and forth and fidgeted in her seat, wrung her hands, and fiddled with her hair. If the hospital staff hadn't already left for the day, she would have gone over there right then.

Silence settled over them as Yehya sank deeper into his turbulent thoughts. He knew there was no other way forward, but he'd been to Zephyr Hospital once in his life and it had been enough; he knew how dangerous it would be for Amani to go on her own, particularly at a time like this. Things had become increasingly restrictive, and her visit might draw more attention to him, resulting in his X-ray vanishing from that hospital as well. His options flickered and faded in front of him, he was losing one after another. He rested his elbows on the table and sank his forehead into his palms. The mention of Zephyr Hospital reminded him of the doctor in military uniform who'd asked about him at the office a while back.

Amani didn't have any more information than she'd written in her letter; the man had arrived mysteriously and was gone within minutes. He hadn't left a business card or phone number, nothing but the name of the place where he worked, which was now engraved in her mind.

Nagy tried to break the silence casually and mentioned that Ehab had offered to go with Amani—actually, he'd insisted on it. Like Yehya, he was cautious around Amani's harsh temper that was quick to flare up, and he expected her to be annoyed by Ehab's insistence, afraid he might jeopardize the whole plan. But although she remained tense, she didn't get angry. She was less concerned with Ehab and more afraid of anything that might ruin this opportunity. She had become Yehya's only hope when all other ways forward were blocked. She knew that their success depended on her making her visit to the hospital seem routine and innocent, just an ordinary request. She had to act in a way that would make asking the hospital official for an X-ray seem entirely unimportant, not alarming at all, the kind of request that plenty of people had made before her without any complication.

Amani agreed that Ehab could come, but she stressed to Nagy that as long as she didn't run into any problems, Ehab had to keep his distance from her, and he could only interfere if it was absolutely necessary. The tension in their conversation eased, and Yehya asked her to avoid the doctor from Zephyr who had come to the office, who was bound to recognize her face.

Amani paid the bill, easily beating them to the check; she was the only one among them who still had a steady job and reliable income. Nagy sat gazing out the window at the coffee shop across the road while Yehya headed to the toilet. While there, he carefully inspected his underwear, and then pulled it up after counting the concentric circles of blood. There were two fresh rings. He put his head under the tap, let the water run over him, and caught up with the others by the door.

With every piece of news that another citizen had disappeared, Ines grew more anxious. She wouldn't leave her place for more than a moment, and Um Mabrouk began to send Mabrouk to bring her breakfast every day, so she wouldn't pass out from hunger. Ines never imagined she would fall victim to fear like this, having long considered herself one of the most resolute and resilient of people. She'd lived alone in a big apartment for years, had gotten through university and finished her studies in peace without anyone to look after her, and then had applied for jobs and been the first in her class to get one. She skillfully surpassed the other women in her cohort; she was hired first, given a permanent position first, and given a better bonus. She was known for her flawless teaching reputation, beloved by her students and their parents alike, who were always impressed by her dedication.

Yet despite this spotless record, things had changed overnight. Her first mistake had brought her to the Gate against her will, and she didn't know where she'd end up as a result of the second one. Soon she might be no more than a note in the margins of the escalating unemployment figures. She was haunted by waking dreams, imagining a photograph of herself in a turquoise headscarf printed on one of the missing-person flyers, which her mother would distribute in the queue and pass sorrowfully among the people waiting.

Her parents would never forgive her if her mother had to

return from the Gulf because of her, if she was the reason they lost their jobs and their good salary in riyals. And if Ines tarnished the family name, it could result in divorce for her sister, who would be forced to leave her husband's house and take her children with her. She would blame Ines for everything she'd done, even though it hadn't been intentional. Not even in her worst nightmares had she seen things ending up like this. She'd never meant to make disparaging remarks about Shalaby, his cousin, or the guard unit he belonged to. If she had known that the exchange would be transmitted to officials behind the Gate, just the mention of his name would have given her chills, she would've never opened her mouth in the first place, and she wouldn't have ignored Um Mabrouk's advice.

THE HIGH SHEIKH

The boycott against Violet Telecom suffered a harsh blow at the hands of the High Sheikh, who issued a fatwa declaring it impermissible to harm the economic interests of the country and its people. It also criminalized boycotts that negatively affected businesses owned by God-fearing believers. The fatwa declared that if anyone insulted religion in any way, boycotting and ignoring them would be not only permissible but also a religious duty. It concluded by saying that believers should continue to treat their brothers charitably, even if in doing so it brought them hardship or put them in danger.

The man in the *galabeya* was the first to embrace the High Sheikh's fatwa: he took a microphone, stood alongside the queue, and read the statement aloud from a copy in his hand. He'd turned off his phone and placed it in his inner breast pocket so it wouldn't attract attention; the woman with the short hair had recently accused him, in front of everyone, of discrediting the boycott campaign to defend Violet Telecom, while secretly using another phone network himself. She had discovered that he hadn't been affected by Violet Telecom's surveillance measures at all, and—more significantly—that he owned a large amount of stock in the company.

After concluding his slow and deliberate reading, he announced enthusiastically that he would dedicate his next weekly lesson to "God's will," to introduce people to fatwas and explain their importance. He urged people who had joined the boycott campaign to attend his lecture, to listen and make use of what he said, and he secretly hoped that God would let him be the one to inspire them to turn away from temptation and embrace the truth.

Ehab didn't hear the fatwa, but before long he found a copy on a faded slip of paper with tattered edges.

From the Fatwa and Rationalizations Committee, on the Fifth Day of this Venerable Month:

In light of its meeting today, the Committee hereby announces this fatwa to the entire nation, to ward off civil strife and its evils, and preserve the country's integrity. To keep those of faith from succumbing to sin in the eyes of God Almighty, all believers must verify any news before giving it credence, and all those who make claims must substantiate their assertions with proof, lest they spread false allegations and therefore corruption. Believers shall not boycott their brothers, nor cause them to suffer financial or emotional distress, and shall not call upon others to take such actions, as this is one of the gravest sins, unless done in support of religion. A believer who is weak of faith, and does not join his brothers, is guilty of a sin, which shall be weighed on Judgment Day. This sin can be absolved by fasting, or by making seven consecutive phone calls, each one not separated by more than a month. Our Book pronounces this truth upon you. May God lead you to the path of righteousness, and may His peace, blessings, and mercy be upon you.

[The High Sheikh's signature, and an illegible date]

Ehab folded the paper up and put it in his notebook, and then wrote the time of the lesson on the last page, the one filled with lists of numbers and dates and names. He walked off, determined to attend the lesson and record what wisdom the man in the *galabeya* would bestow upon his disciples. He wondered how the man would answer their questions, and Ehab's own, which he also wrote in his notebook, underlining several times the ones he considered most important.

After opening prayers, appeals for protection from Satan and his vile machinations, and entreaties that his supporters be spared eternal damnation, the man in the *galabeya* began a rousing discourse. He spoke of the need to verify every word one utters, and insisted that a believer's behavior and decisions could not be built upon doubt. He didn't say a word without supporting it with passages from the scripture, and he won most people over, especially those who had come from beyond the queue for the first time. Many wept during the lesson, including Um Mabrouk. She realized that much of her bad luck wasn't due to God's anger with her personally, but with humanity as a whole, due to those who had forsaken religion's teachings, and given in to Satan's whispers. She cried harder as the man sonorously recited a passage from the Greater Book that cautioned against telling untruths about others or passing on false rumors, and when he explained the passage, she felt that his speech was meant for her. Her tears streamed down her face, and she swore to herself repentantly that she'd abandon the cell-phone boycott and instead only blacklist the candy factory, since she'd seen with her own eyes the candies that Shalaby had destroyed. The man in the *galabeya* imparted some of his own theological opinions on the fatwa, too. He said it was the right of a father—and those of a father's rank and position—to watch over his children, using all available means. This could not be considered an infringement of their privacy, he added, and ended his speech by saying that honest citizens had nothing to hide from their guardians.

Ines appeared at the end of the lesson wearing a loose white veil that fell halfway down her stomach, concealing her breasts. After people had dispersed from the front of the queue and crowded around the man, she tried to pass on the lesson's advice to the woman with the short hair, who stood watching from a distance. She hoped to dissuade her from continuing the campaign, but wasn't met with any success. The woman with the short hair redoubled her efforts, and the next day she printed oppositional leaflets responding to the allegations made by the man in the *galabeya*, and declared that she would continue the campaign. Ehab had helped her draft the text, and alongside her statement they'd included another passage from the Greater Book, which urged people to respect and defend personal privacy. He wrote a hard-hitting and well-researched article about the campaign—its grounds and implications, and how many people joined each week—but the newspaper didn't print it. Instead, they gave him a stern warning about "fabricating the news." The editor in chief lectured him on how necessary it was to strive for accuracy and honesty in everything he wrote. Then he warned Ehab against giving in to ambition and trying to achieve professional or financial gains at the expense of journalistic ethics and principles.

The man in the *galabeya* intensified his lessons in response to the leaflets, making each lesson longer than the last. Shortly afterward, he was overheard speaking on his cell phone, while picking at the toes of his right foot, repeating that he'd done all he could. He told the person on the other end that he wanted to buy a horse and ride up and down the queue, from north to south, so he could give several lessons a day. He could disseminate the fatwa, temper the influence of the woman with the short hair, and achieve a greater heavenly reward. He was also heard confirming that the ban on cars entering the street would stay in place for months, perhaps even years, and lamenting that his feet didn't allow him to walk very far.

FIVE

Document No. 5

The Gate's Response

Tarek spent many fitful nights experimenting with all sorts of sedatives and sleeping pills until his colleagues commented on the dangerous quantities he was requesting from the pharmacy. He ignored them, his mind still preoccupied with Yehya's fate, so consumed by his predicament that at one point he swallowed half a strip of pills in one go. But still, he couldn't sleep. Sabah, who was temporarily managing the nurses, noticed his distress and took it upon herself to keep him away from patients, especially on the days when he arrived at the hospital with dark circles under his eyes. She watched him surreptitiously, and then went to him and reminded him of that strange official visit he'd received the morning after the Disgraceful Events. She revealed that she knew a lot about his patient, the one named Yehya Gad el-Rab Saeed—quite a lot, in fact. But despite all that she knew, she'd chosen to keep her mouth shut and his secret safe. Now she held something over him. She knew that if he noticed any misbehavior from her after that, he wouldn't dare mention it. It was in their mutual interest to work together, for one to erase the other's tracks.

Sabah immediately took advantage of Tarek's leniency toward her. She left work early that day, while Tarek headed to the plush sofa in the corner of his office, stretched out, and closed his eyes. He plunged into a desperate struggle for sleep, pressing against the back of the sofa, then turning over and facing it, bending his knees and curling into a fetal position, then flipping onto his back, stretching his legs over the armrest, and staring up at the ceiling. When met with failure, as he was every time he tried to sleep now, he got up. He went over to his desk, picked up the key to the bottom drawer, and pulled out the file. Its papers were worn and tattered from how often he'd handled them.

The fifth document contained nothing more than a large box as long and wide as the page itself, yellow like all the other pages. It didn't contain a single word and remained empty and pristine. So many times he'd hoped to open the file and find a sentence or two printed there, the way all the other papers he read over and over were inexplicably updated. But he knew that this one would remain blank, would wait for Yehya to receive either a permit to remove the bullet or an official rejection. A permit for the operation was practically hopeless at this point. And if he received a rejection, the file would be closed and sealed with red tape forever.

The box merged with the Gate in his mind, the resemblance overpowering. Vast and vague, able to contain so much. Everything in his world was determined by the Gate, bound to its decisions. His future depended on it, as did Yehya's life, his friends' lives, the lives of countless others. Whether he slept or lay awake, was unperturbed or miserable, everything depended on the Gate—even his work, which had been affected by the closure of the radiology department. And now Sabah was blackmailing him, forcing him into line with her. There was no question that life was more restrictive now, though they'd promised the exact opposite when the Gate first appeared and everyone had rejoiced. They'd said the Gate was going to make everything easier, that it would bring peace, joy, and security to each and every citizen. He was a citizen, a dutiful one, too, but now it was clear that these promises had been empty. The space on the page grew wider before his eyes, encompassing him, as if to swallow him whole and imprison him within it. His head dropped and his eyelids began to close, and then he impulsively turned the paper over, buried his head in his arms, and fell asleep.

ZEPHYR HOSPITAL

Amani woke up early. She picked out a plain pair of jeans and a jacket that wouldn't draw attention, but she was also careful not to look as if she were poor or in a precarious situation. Public officials had a distaste for serving people poor like themselves, even in a hospital like Zephyr, where things should have been different. Standing before the mirror, she rehearsed the manner she used with customers at work, settled on a tone that would sway the official, and practiced a small, friendly smile on her thin lips. Reassured by her appearance, she left the apartment.

A guard from the Concealment Force stopped her at the hospital doors and asked for her ID. He directed her to the Investigations and Instructions Desk, where she left her ID card and took a temporary one. She headed to the main sign with its list of names and arrows, and from there toward the surgery department, following signs that led her down a long corridor with exits to other departments branching off on both sides.

The floor was covered with what looked like rubber; it was dark and an indeterminate color, and the ceiling loomed high above her. The dull gray walls almost seemed to hold the shadows of people who had passed before her, and appeared even more imposing as they towered above her. She felt a coldness in the air, and shivers rippled through her body despite the sweat that was beginning to form along her hairline. Several doctors in white coats with distinctive badges walked past her whispering, but she didn't see the doctor who had visited her at the office, and was reassured a little by this. She looked behind her; she was the only one in the corridor. The last sign pointed toward the surgery department, and she turned down the corridor, then continued until she reached the secretary's office, where she stopped and summoned all the courage she possessed.

She stood before the official in silence; he was busy with a thick notebook open in front of him. Her eyes swept over the writing on the forms, searching for a word about Yehya, but she wasn't used to reading upside down. He noticed her attempts and closed the book quickly, and raising his hand at her, he asked what she wanted by standing there. Her quick, forced smile seemed to have no effect.

"Good morning. I need a copy of an X-ray that was brought here about two months ago."

"What's your name?"

"Actually, it's not under my name, it's for Yehya Gad el-Rab Saeed."

"What's the relation?"

"He's my cousin—my mother's sister's son."

"Do you have authorization to pick it up?"

"I don't, actually . . . I lost it."

"We can't just hand over an X-ray to anyone who walks in here. Not even if belongs to him, not without authorization."

"But he really needs it, the doctor asked him for it, said he needed to get it, as quickly as possible, and it's so hard for him to wait for another X-ray, there are so many people ahead of him, and he'll have to wait maybe a whole month until he gets his turn . . . Please, will you help? I'll do anything."

He looked at her with disinterest, and then opened the notebook again and looked through the names. He asked her if she could remember the date Yehya was admitted, give or take a week or two. She could, but when he searched again he realized that the time period she'd told him included four days that hadn't been entered in the book. His eyes narrowed, almost maliciously, and he stood up and reached over to a huge cabinet. With difficulty, he removed a medium-size file wedged between the massive folders and ran his finger down a list of names on the front.

"His name is here. He was injured in the Disgraceful Events. You should have said that from the start."

"I just came for the X-ray, to be honest, that's all . . . I don't know anything about anything else . . . Do you think I could have it? Please?"

"Of course not. First of all, you need a special form, particularly in cases like this, signed by the doctor who treated him here, and then you have to bring me authorization from the director himself, stamped by him and by the hospital. And secondly, *ya madam*, I don't have the X-ray. It's in the filing department on the fifth floor, and just so you know, no one's permitted up there."

The color had left her face; the official knew how Yehya had been injured. Her attempt at naïveté had failed, but she maintained her composure, refusing to be defeated so quickly, and decided to see it through to the end. She asked him for the name of the doctor attending to Yehya's case and where he could be found. He ripped a scrap of paper from the corner of a roll that happened to be nearby, scribbled something down, folded it, and held it out to her. He bade her goodbye with a mocking glare, and she hurried away. She didn't open the piece of paper until she was far from the window and sure she was no longer in range of his sneering gaze, which felt like it pierced right through her. *Dr. Safwat Kamel Abdel Azeem— Fourth Floor, Special Cases.* She put the scrap of paper in the inside pocket of her purse and took out her cell phone, and saw several missed calls, all from the same number. She called the number back, and an unfamiliar voice picked up on the other end.

"Amani? It's Ehab, Yehya and Nagy's friend. Are you okay?"

"I'm fine. Perfect timing, though. Are you in the hospital?"

"I'm out front. Do you need any help?"

"I think so."

"Right, I'll meet you at the entrance. I'm wearing a light-blue shirt and sunglasses, and I'll be holding a newspaper."

Amani quickened her pace back along the corridor to the lobby. She felt a sense of relief to no longer be dealing with this alone. She watched the entrance from afar, pretending to be talking on the phone so that none of the staff would ask her what she was doing or offer to show her how she may have strayed. Ehab appeared a few minutes later. He walked over to the Investigations and Instructions Desk and showed them his ID card, but after standing in front of the official for what seemed like an age, he became obviously exasperated with the conversation. Amani began to worry, and her heart beat faster when she saw Ehab tussle with the man and the other officials behind the counter.

She watched several guards rush over, shouting at Ehab, and they didn't lead him away so much as carry him by his hands and feet to the hospital door before throwing him out. A tinny announcement echoed through the lobby, broadcast over the intercom on repeat, asking for her, Amani Sayed

Ibrahim, to come to the Investigations and Instructions Desk immediately. She was now back at square one, or maybe even square zero. The Concealment Force was trained to catch people trying to infiltrate the place, and if she responded to the announcement, they would throw her out, too. Wildly, she wished the official would change his mind and let her have the X-ray, whether out of sympathy or complicity, but she knew that was impossible. She needed to act decisively, fearlessly. She didn't have time to weigh her options, and there was no way of knowing what was best. She abandoned the idea that Ehab would return and pushed hope of the official's sudden kindness far from her mind. If she wanted the X-ray, she would have to get it on her own.

She looked around. No one was following her, and she walked toward the elevator as the announcement was repeated for the tenth time. She pushed the button and slowly stepped out onto the fifth floor when the doors opened. Her eyes wandered across the large, barren space, which looked like it had been emptied of everything it had once contained. No people, no chairs, not even signs like those she'd followed on the ground floor, past hospital wards, offices, and officials. Nothing at all. She studied the high ceiling as the elevator doors rolled into motion and closed behind her. There was a doorway connected to the lobby, and she cautiously slipped through it and walked through the narrow corridors until she noticed a closed door. This, she suddenly realized, was what she had come for. Next to the door was a pink plaque made of some strange, shiny metal, and engraved on it were the words DEPARTMENT OF CRITICAL BULLET FILES. She grabbed the cold metal door handle, but there wasn't enough time; the elevator opened again and angry voices clamored over one another. She couldn't understand a thing they were saying, but she recognized a face in the confusion, the one face she'd hoped never to see at a moment like this.

Ehab tried to get back into Zephyr, but it was impossible. They had posted an enlarged photocopy of his ID card at the entrance and distributed it to the Concealment Force. He headed to the newspaper headquarters, where he met his editor and filled him in on what had happened, and then he set off for the queue in search of Nagy. He didn't want to tell Yehya what had happened because he didn't want to worry him, especially as Ehab didn't have anything reassuring to say. After the scuffle in the lobby and being thrown out of the hospital, he had nothing good to report, and now Amani's phone wasn't in service, either. He and Nagy left the queue together, unseen by Yehya, and headed to Amani's apartment. They knocked on her door for nearly a quarter of an hour, until the *bawab* came up to say he hadn't seen her since that morning. She was probably still at work, the old doorman said, and he invited them to wait with him in front of the building until she returned.

They sat with the *bawab* for a long time as he made tea, took a few cigarettes out of his pocket and placed them in front of them, and then told them about the building he'd guarded since he was a boy. When he first arrived, the district had been a vast and remote expanse, there were no other buildings or people—just this one, its residents, and the desert beyond. The closest inhabited district was a few miles down the highway. But the place he had known had vanished long ago. High-rise buildings sprouted, scores of people marched in and settled down, markets opened up, and the area was now bursting at the seams. He let out a grievous sigh and gestured off into the distance with a veiny hand, saying that there was still one empty plot of land out there, vacant and vast. Ehab got excited, as he knew the land the doorman was referring to: it was now under the Gate's dominion. The old man laughed and coughed, spouting a puff of smoke, and added that although many years had gone by, people were still reluctant to buy there because of its past. Everyone knew what had once stood there: a detention center from which those who'd entered never returned, not even after decades.

The old man said the area had changed a great deal since the Gate appeared, and even more so after it had closed and the queue formed nearby. Back when the Gate had still been open, there was always a huge commotion during working hours, with people shouting. But when its work ended, it became deathly still, and not a single voice was heard, as if no one had ever gone in and no one ever left. As time passed, he told them, people said the weather in the area was always strangely stifling—but only around the Gate—and that sometimes the sun both rose *and set* over the Northern Building, perhaps bowing to whatever went on in there. People passing by it became increasingly wary and didn't even act like themselves when they were nearby, especially after the Disgraceful Events.

He leaned in a little closer, having decided he could trust them, and whispered that Amani had gone to Zephyr Hospital, that Zephyr Hospital belonged to the Gate, and that he had suspicions about her work, and about her involvement in those Events people talked about. On the night after the Events she hadn't returned home until after midnight, which was unusual for her, and on more than one occasion people from strange organizations had come asking about her, although they'd never asked to speak to her directly.

They waited all day in front of her building, but Amani had vanished. Nagy and Ehab returned to the queue to look for Yehya, filled with a greater sense of helplessness than ever before. They both felt guilty that they hadn't been with Amani from the start. When Um Mabrouk heard the news, she immediately decided to distribute leaflets; Abbas designed them in exchange for a few free phone calls, wafers, and juice, and signed it at the bottom as usual. He made copies at a nearby photocopier, whose owner owed him a favor, and gave her a hundred copies. The flyer featured an old photo of Amani, since Um Mabrouk didn't have a recent one. Abbas had written her full name with great care, followed by the standard wording for these kinds of cases: an appeal to the Gate to intervene, find the person, and investigate the strange circumstances around the disappearance. Um Mabrouk put the flyers next to her wares, wailing and lamenting her eternal bad luck, and explaining—even in the absence of customers—that Amani was like a daughter to her. When she'd buried her elder daughter the day after she died, Amani had come from so far, cried like no one had ever cried before, and hadn't even gone home until the funeral was finished and all the lights were out.

NOTHING

The man questioned her about her name, age, marital status, education, profession, and place of residence, but it was clear that he already knew all the answers. Then he leaned back from the desk and asked what Amani was doing on the fifth floor when she knew it was a restricted area. She tried to remain as calm and polite as possible, and apologized. She wasn't familiar with the place, she said, she just wanted to pick up her cousin's X-ray, and was running late for their meeting with the doctor. He was bound to come looking for her, and would tell her family, she added, who no doubt were worried sick because she hadn't called. Amani was standing in the middle of the room with the pink sign, where they'd brought her once they'd found her. The room was filled with files stacked so high that she couldn't see the walls. She had a vague sense of fear and the feeling that she was somewhere she shouldn't be, but she trusted that she could talk her way out, and her thoughts remained firmly on Yehya and helping him. The man said nothing. Someone she couldn't see came up from behind her and stopped in front of him, addressing him with effusive respect.

"Safwat *basha*, there aren't any files under the name Yehya Gad el-Rab Saeed here, sir."

"That should be sufficient for you," he said to Amani. "We have no files under that name here, so don't go troubling yourself and troubling me, too."

"But I know he was transferred here to Zephyr Hospital, and left two days later."

"Excellent. Then clearly he had no reason to stick around, and no need for treatment."

She raised her voice in response; his comment had provoked her, and she grew angry when she realized he was enjoying toying with her.

"No, there was a lot he needed—there was a bullet in his pelvis, a bullet from when he was shot during the Disgraceful Events."

The stony-faced man rose from his seat, tall and broad, and then slammed his fist down on the desk with a loud crack. The files shook on their shelves and some fell to the floor.

"No one was injured by any bullet that day or the day after or on any other day, do you understand?"

She took a step back, but she'd lost her temper. Her self-control crumbled, and she shouted back at him.

"Lies! He's wounded, and the bullet is still in his body, and as soon as they do the operation and he has the bullet in his hand he'll tell everyone who shot him, and then you'll have your proof!"

Silence hung in the air, she heard only the pounding of her heart, while the veins on both sides of her forehead swelled and shivers ran up and down her arms. She was breathing hard, as if poised to defend herself from an impending attack.

Nothingness. She wasn't blindfolded, but all she could see was black. She moved her palms away from her face . . . nothing. She heard no voices, her hands felt no walls, no columns, no bars. She saw and felt nothing, only the solid earth underneath her, where she stood or sat or slept. Perhaps she was only earth, too. She walked in every direction but met nothing but a void. She tried to scream, to be silent and listen out for other voices, to swear and curse every person who deserved to be punished for wronging her. Or even just name them. The Gate and the people who ran it. Violet Telecom. The High Sheikh. And then she took it all back and asked for forgiveness, rebelling then pleading, filled with courage then wracked with tears. But everything remained as it was: nothingness.

She didn't know how she'd arrived in this emptiness, how time was passing, or whether it was passing at all. Again and again, she tried to let sleep wash over her, so that she would wake from this nothingness. She wanted to wake up to something else, anything else but this. She wanted to see color or just a single point of light, even if it were only in her dreams, but her dreams failed her, even her daydreams. First the color drained from her imagination, then so did the light, so that her mind too became black. Gradually, she began to forget faces: her mother's, Yehya's, her boss's. The familiar details of their faces became blurry until they were featureless. Was it possible that her own memory was being stolen from her? That she would lose forever the images that had lived in her mind for so long? She had nothing to touch but her own body, could hear nothing but her own voice when she let out a sound. All she had was this strange ground. It didn't have the coldness of stone, or the feel of wood when she walked on it, or the texture of carpet or any other material. She bent down and brought her nose close to it, but it had no scent either; she realized she couldn't smell it, couldn't smell anything, not even her sweat, or her clothes. What had happened to her clothes? She was no longer wearing her jeans or her jacket, didn't have her purse. Was it possible that they'd taken her off the face of the earth, out into space, and had left her naked on a dark, uninhabited planet? What had happened to her before she'd woken up and found herself here? She opened her eyes, first one then the other, prying them open with her fingers, then she touched her thighs and her breasts and in between her legs, checking they hadn't . . . She shouted and shouted, she swore she would never oppose them again, she pleaded for forgiveness, and then out of desperation she promised she wouldn't see Yehya again. She felt her body trembling and the muscles of her face contract. Things would never go back to how they were. She tried to open her mouth, struggling, and then said that she'd lied. She admitted that he wasn't her cousin, he wasn't waiting for her, wasn't going to tell her family, she didn't even have a family. But still nothing. With every moment that passed she was drawing closer to the edge of collapse. She couldn't put together a rational thought anymore, or come up with possibilities, not the way she'd always been able to. It felt as though time had paused, and dropped her into a well of madness.

She wished they would beat her, she said she was ready to be tortured, she slapped her face with her hands until her cheekbones went numb, and bit her lips to feel her own blood inside her mouth but she tasted nothing. Nothing, again. Maybe she really was nothing, had never existed. Or maybe she would disintegrate here, slowly dissolving until she became nothingness . . . became nothing. She was already beginning to disappear: her tears were the first part of her to vanish. She tried to resist it; she squeezed her eyes shut, she thought about dying there to make herself cry, but the tears didn't come. They had disappeared. Evaporated. The first part of her had vanished;

the rest would follow. She sat and wrapped her arms around herself, waiting to disappear completely.

Yehya was distraught for days. Every morning and evening he left the queue and walked to Amani's apartment, and despite the aching pain in his side, he spent hours searching the nearby streets and looking for her in the crowds. Nagy forbade him from going to Zephyr Hospital, convincing him there was nothing to be gained. If he went, he too would disappear, the bullet inside him would be lost, and everything that he'd endured in those past months would've been for nothing. Yehya knew that Amani was strong and would hold her ground, but he also knew her courage gave way to recklessness when she was angry, which inevitably got her into more trouble. Ehab's newspaper printed a notice, but it was brief and vague; Um Mabrouk ran out of flyers within hours, and though Shalaby volunteered to ask his fellow guards in his old Servant Force unit about the fate of people who'd disappeared recently, none of their answers made sense to him, and none of them could help.

She left in the early morning, or rather, she didn't leave but found herself in a tunnel. She followed the tunnel all the way until it let out, not far from the Booth. From there she walked to the main road, and then she took a microbus. She got off far from home and walked the rest of the way, climbing the steps to her building in silence so that the doorman wouldn't notice her. Nothing had changed. Her clothes were still there, her shoes strewn on the floor where she'd left them, the pan in the sink, the half-eaten egg sandwich on the table going stale.

Her senses seemed to be working again, but she needed to be sure. She opened the freezer and was hit with a mix of smells, she peeled garlic, turned on every light in the apartment and examined the wool carpet on the floor, allowing her eyes to absorb all its colors. Finally she tentatively approached the big mirror in her bathroom. She held back, scared of looking into it and finding just a dark shadow of herself. She looked down at her palms, flipped her hands over, spread her fingers and her toes. Then suddenly she leapt forward toward the mirror, as if diving into the sea. She saw her face: haggard and gray but whole, her eyes and nose and mouth, her hair; it was her.

In her purse she found a stack of photographs. There was a photo of her rushing toward Yehya as he was shot down, and a photo of her in the second round of clashes, the ones that the Gate had denied had ever happened. In that photo she was running through the Restricted Zone, and they had captured her face so clearly that there could be no doubt that it was her. In another photo she was with Yehya and Nagy in the cafeteria, the dish of *fuul* beans in front of her. There were so many photos of her every movement and she had no idea who had taken them. But nothing surprised her anymore. The last picture was completely black, as if exposed while being developed, and she mused that despite such sophisticated surveillance they were still using film cameras.

Amani didn't leave the house for a week after she returned; she didn't go to work and she didn't pick up the phone. It was the *bawab* who called Um Mabrouk, and after asking how her children were doing, he told her that Amani had returned. The lights from her living room shone down into the light well where he slept, and they'd been on since the day before yesterday. A garbage bin had appeared outside her apartment door, too. At first he'd doubted it was her, but then she gave him his monthly payment herself. Before she had even hung up the phone, Um Mabrouk let out a *zaghrouta* of joy, the first the queue had ever heard.

They all came to visit, but Amani was tired and didn't sit with them for long. She didn't say much, and spoke without emotion or enthusiasm. When they asked her what had happened, she told them that the guards from the Concealment Force had grown suspicious when they found her looking for the X-ray, so they'd stopped her and detained her for a while. They confiscated her cell phone, examined her ID card, and questioned her about why she was there, but then let her go. She said she'd come home on the verge of a bad cold, something she'd most likely caught at the hospital, and had been in bed with a fever and sore throat. That was why she hadn't answered the phone. She pointed to a pile of boxes of medicine and pills on the coffee table. She hadn't found the X-ray in Zephyr, she added, and was now convinced it had never been sent there in the first place. Tarek must have lost it, and misled them to avoid responsibility. Nagy nodded without a word, while Yehya fell still. Ehab stood up from his chair, saying that they should go and give her a chance to rest. They would come back when she was feeling better, and for now they needed to figure out what to do next.

She closed the door behind them and went back to the living room, wishing that her headache would leave, too. She carried the cups to the kitchen and washed them slowly, letting the minutes go by, her mind elsewhere. The sound of the cups and the feel of the water had a calming effect that she had never appreciated before. She dried the cups and put them on the shelf, and left the room without turning off the lights.

None of them said a word as they left, because there was no need to say what they were all thinking: Amani was hiding something. It was possible that the guards had humiliated or threatened her, or even beaten her. But she didn't appear to have been hurt and there were no signs of violence on her body. Something had happened but there was no way of knowing what it was. Maybe they had used their mysterious methods to extract information from her about Yehya and the evidence they were trying so hard to cover up. Or to find out information on Nagy, without whom Yehya would not still be alive, or Ehab, about whom they already knew so much, far more than Amani would have been able to tell them. Or perhaps they hadn't interrogated her at all; maybe they had just scared her by playing with her emotions and deepest secrets, and that had been enough to strip her of all her natural vitality and determination, leaving her in this dull and lifeless state, not like herself at all.

As they walked back to the queue, Yehya saw an old building with SPECIAL ANALYSIS AND SCANS written on its side, and left them, slowly crossing the road to examine it. The door was locked and bound with a rusty metal chain. There was no point trying to enter; the new decree was in effect everywhere now, and even small clinics and hospitals couldn't escape it. He looked around again and then gestured to Nagy and Ehab across the street, pointing to a big pharmacy. He disappeared for a moment and emerged with a box of painkillers. A few blocks later, they passed a small phone shop that Yehya used to stop at, whenever he was thinking of buying a new phone. He asked the shopkeeper about the prices of phone plans and handsets, and the man told him about a couple of offers and then produced an elegant violet box, with the Violet Telecom logo emblazoned on the front. Yehya turned it down, asking for any other brand, but the man apologized, explaining that the entire shop had been sold to the company, and that he would soon be changing the sign in front, too.

THE OFFICE

After their surprise visit, Amani answered her phone only once, despite how often they all called her. Her voice had been faint and her words disjointed, and she'd begged Nagy to be patient with her. She'd asked him to stop pestering her until she was better and could go back to work, assuring him she would call him from the office. It was clear that she didn't want them to visit her at home, and they began to call her less and less frequently. Cell phones weren't really safe anymore, and people wondered about landlines, too. But she never failed to make one weekly call: to check on Yehya, to make sure his situation hadn't deteriorated, and to reassure him, however unconvincingly, that she was well. Yehya was dispirited, and worry seemed to have aged him. The patches of blood on his clothes grew steadily larger; he was bleeding all the time now, no longer just when he urinated, and growing weaker from the loss of blood.

Yehya wanted to give Amani some space and the freedom to come to him when she felt ready to tell him what was haunting her. But when he didn't hear from her for two weeks, he abandoned his hesitation and decided to limp his way to the office in the hope that she'd returned to work. His old boss greeted him coolly, despite how close they had been when Yehya was an employee. He'd worked there for nearly ten years, and in that time had brought in a significant number of new clients and had been responsible for huge increases in their sales, but his past performance did him no good now. The director spoke to him with a mixture of distrust and annoyance, and grumbled when he asked about Amani. Yehya thought that if his old boss hadn't felt too guilty to say so, he would have told him not to stay long, or asked him why he was there at all.

He found Amani in their old office. He was comforted by the fact that it was just as he remembered it, with the broken fan still dangling from the ceiling as it always had. The only change was the absence of the lace curtain, which had fallen to the floor and now lay on the drab, grimy carpet. Amani was distraught and ashen-faced, and on her desk were piles of papers and lists of customer's names and numbers, as though she'd let them pile up for months. He pulled out a chair, slowly and with difficulty, and reached out to take her hand. It was cold and trembling. When she finally realized that it really was Yehya in front of her, and not just a figment of her troubled imagination, she took his hand between hers and squeezed it hard, as if it might rescue her.

She asked numerous questions about his health, if he had any updates about his operation, and about the blood that now stained his clothes day and night. She gave him her full attention, listened to him intently, and asked for more news until he had nothing more to tell her and had exhausted the stories circling in his head. He intentionally kept a few details from her; she was worried enough about him as it was. He carried the burden of having exposed her to danger the night he was injured, and the burden of whatever it was that she still did not dare mention.

When it was her turn to talk, she balked and stalled, offering only muddled words. A desperate look came over her, and suddenly she looked like she was very far away. He placed his hands on her shoulders, filled with concern, and she turned and looked at him blankly. Only the slightest hint of her spirit was left, and he could tell that she saw the worry on his face.

"It's nothing, Yehya. Nothing happened to me. I was just remembering something, something stupid."

The director walked past the room and paused in front of the door. Yehya stood up to leave, and tenderly patted the back of her hand before whispering a few words into her ear. She shook her head at him, and smiled faintly.

INES

Shalaby asked Hammoud to show him the article in the news-paper. He'd heard the newscaster read it on television while he was sitting in the coffee shop, and felt as if he'd found a light shining out of the gloom. Hammoud picked up the newspaper and opened it to the page with the article, and Shalaby asked him to cut it out for him so that he could keep it. He spread the clipping among his things on the table, careful not to tear or crumple it. Then he took a final gulp of his tea and rushed off back to the queue.

Shalaby was still angry with Ines for what she'd said about his cousin Mahfouz; she'd insulted him, and Shalaby had been waiting to get his revenge. Her words hadn't left his mind, and he gnashed his teeth in anguish as he remembered their conversation. He blamed himself for not giving her the response she deserved, and now he felt as though his words were tainted. Every time he told his story he glanced around, looking for her, afraid she would butt in like last time, ruining it and turning him into the laughingstock of the queue.

He had to admit that she'd really riled him from the moment he had arrived in the queue, even if she was only a woman. She was just one person out of dozens, hundreds even, one against a whole village, but she was still just a woman—and one who didn't know her place. She thought she was so smart, but he knew more than she did. He had heard things from behind the scenes, from people who knew things, that the young man Mahfouz had killed had been a believer, who'd prayed and fasted and went to mosque on Fridays, and that he probably wasn't a rioter, just a passerby. But surely Mahfouz hadn't known this. They said that the young man had been on his way to work, but Mahfouz had also been working, just obeying orders. Mahfouz had wanted nothing more than to complete his service as soon as he could and return home; his cousins had moved recently, and he planned to join them.

Yehya arrived at the queue as Shalaby was returning from the coffee shop. Despite the pain, he felt blissful. In his mind he held the first gentle smile that had crossed Amani's lips since she'd disappeared. Now that he'd seen her, he felt a faint flickering of hope suddenly glowing inside him, giving him the will to keep fighting. She'd agreed to see him again and now the world was different, almost brighter. True, she hadn't revealed anything new or confessed what pained her, or eased his concerns about how wary she had become. If anything, she'd confirmed his fears that he wouldn't find out what had happened to her, at least not until the Gate opened and resolved this overwhelming situation. But she'd given him permission to visit her at work, and that was all that mattered. Even if only rarely, he could be near her again. Next time, they would have cinnamon tea together, with milk, just the way she liked it. They'd go out to dinner like they used to do, and he wouldn't say so much, to stop time rushing by as it had today. He would let her tell him this secret when she wanted to, without pressuring her.

Suddenly, Shalaby's rough hand reached out in front of Yehya, startling him, rupturing his reverie. Shalaby was fishing out leaflets from his old frayed leather bag and distributing them to everyone around him. Yehya saw that it was an article photocopied from *The Truth*. Ehab grabbed one eagerly, and another landed in Um Mabrouk's hands, but when she realized that there weren't any pictures she could understand, she passed it to Ines, who had become so skittish lately that she flinched. When Ines realized that everyone else was holding the same thing, she accepted a copy cautiously. "MASTER-MIND OF THE DISGRACEFUL EVENTS DISCOVERED!" was the article's dramatic headline. There weren't enough papers to go around, so the woman with the short hair volunteered to read a few lines to everyone who had gathered.

> *It has been revealed that a foreign individual, who was accused of terrorism in his home nation and sentenced in absentia to life imprisonment, entered the country several months ago. Assisted by operatives, ingrates, and fools, he plotted to stir up unrest and destroy the trust between the Gate and the people. It has been reported that this foreign instigator succumbed to a fatal injury last week, before his wicked schemes were accomplished, leaving no information behind. Extensive investigations are now underway to determine the extent of this man's involvement in the Disgraceful Events, as he is believed to have been responsible for the gunfire witnessed in the square during that time.*

Shalaby weaved around the queue to see what reaction the leaflets were getting. He darted here and there, rereading the article: it claimed that the Quell Force, which included the branch that Mahfouz had belonged to, hadn't shot anyone; the Disgraceful Events were simply a conspiracy hatched by some cowardly foreigners and a few measly traitors who had orchestrated the Events by planting seeds of discord among people, intentionally trying to divide them. These traitors and foreigners had framed the guard units (guards like his cousin, thought Shalaby) for the deaths that had occurred during the Events, and then vanished before anyone could suspect them. These conspirators had a long history of concocting plots and schemes just like this one, but God was just, and so their role in the Events had been revealed.

The truth has finally emerged, thought Shalaby, pleased with this new version of events. This meant that Mahfouz was blameless, not guilty of any wrongdoing. It was those rabble-rousers who'd crossed the line, and his cousin the martyr had simply taught them a lesson—using his truncheon. He'd used it before, nearly every day, and according to the experts, truncheon blows never result in death. Mahfouz had had nothing to do with the casualties from the Events, Shalaby told himself; his cousin had probably never even fired a shot. What's more, he thought, it was possible that Mahfouz hadn't even been carrying his truncheon at the time.

Shalaby now had the proof to defend his cousin. Even if skeptics claimed that Mahfouz *had* fired his gun—and even if he had—now they knew that a foreign spy had been shooting, too, so who could say which bullets belonged to whom? Shalaby couldn't verify it himself; he hadn't seen Mahfouz's gun and didn't know whether it was missing a bullet. But he'd heard from other guards that no one had found the bullet that people *claimed* had penetrated the man's skull. The man had been taken to a military hospital and the doctors tried to save his life, they'd even opened up his head. But the doctors said they hadn't removed any bullets—not from the man, not from anyone.

At any rate, the real culprit had finally emerged, and investigations being conducted at that very moment would definitely prove that Shalaby was right. Mahfouz's family deserved a pension, compensation, and recognition. Shalaby's imagination ran wild as he thought about what he would ask for when he got to the Gate. He dreamed of building a memorial in their hometown with the names of all the martyrs, and Mahfouz at the top of the list, so people would always remember that he had died a hero.

Shalaby returned to his place behind Ines and stood there triumphantly, like a military general just back from victory in battle. He puffed out his chest, thoroughly pleased with himself and his new position as the cousin of a martyr. With this newspaper, he had finally been given justice. He'd been watching Ines the whole time he was distributing leaflets, and he'd observed her face carefully to see how she reacted to the news. Even while discussing it with other people, he'd made sure to keep her in view. He'd finally had his say and shut her up for good. After today, he thought, there was no way she'd dare question Mahfouz's honor, or accuse him of turning on his countrymen, or claim that he'd killed someone. She hadn't said a single word. Maybe she'd realized how wrong she was. Maybe she would apologize to him in front of everyone, Shalaby thought eagerly, just as she'd mocked him in front of them all before.

After Ines read the article, her fears multiplied. She knew that her conversation with Shalaby had been recorded: she'd made accusations, called for justice for people she knew were untouchable, and crossed the biggest line. She was definitely going to be arrested, she thought, now that this foreign instigator had been discovered. If anyone found out what she'd said, she'd be charged with spreading lies. They would accuse her of colluding with him, and maybe Shalaby would add the charge that she'd tarnished his cousin's reputation. She was sure to be convicted, and new evidence would probably appear proving that she was connected in some way or another to this "foreign hand," who of course wouldn't be at trial to deny it, since he was dead. She wouldn't just lose her job, or be disappeared for a while; she'd spend the rest of her life in prison, and all the flyers in the world wouldn't be able to help.

Was the paper that Um Mabrouk had stumbled upon the only record of that conversation, and had she unintentionally recovered it? Maybe she should take all possibilities into consideration and search for a lawyer among the people in the queue.

Amid all the debates and discussions that Shalaby had sparked, not a single person was aware of her predicament. She stood firm in her place, nervously fidgeting with her new, more conservative attire, making sure that her neck and hair were completely covered. Then she went to the man in the *galabeya* to ask if she could use his phone, claiming that hers had broken when she'd accidentally dropped it on the ground.

Nagy grabbed Yehya's arm and dragged him away from the people who had gathered around Shalaby and his leaflets. Nagy wasn't concerned with Mahfouz or whether or not he'd actually shot someone. Something in the article had roused a question in his mind. The newspaper acknowledged that bullets had been fired during the Disgraceful Events—did that mean the Gate also acknowledged that people had been injured by gunfire? Or was it still covering that up? The wording was so vague that they had nothing to grasp. They didn't spend long discussing what this might mean for them, and just agreed to forge ahead with their plan, unswayed. Yehya knew where the bullet moving around in his pelvis came from, he'd seen who shot him, and nothing could deny or change that, not as long as he was still alive.

Um Mabrouk gradually secured more space for her stand and set up two plastic chairs in front of her, as well as a big rock she'd dragged over from the sidewalk opposite. With a young man's help, she turned it on its side to make a little table and put out drinks for her favorite customers. She told Mabrouk to collect the newspapers and magazines that people left at the coffee shop, on the street, and around the Booth every day. She also had him collect things that people in the queue didn't need—anything that could provide a bit of distraction and entertainment. She told him to ask around at the front of the queue in particular, as that was where the more distinguished and wealthier people stood.

The woman with the short hair settled next to Um Mabrouk, figuring that the constant flow of customers would be a good opportunity to recruit for the campaign. Her discussions with customers went further, branching out beyond the Violet Telecom boycott to address people's livelihoods and other issues that were affecting them. Meanwhile, her radio, which had been on constantly since she'd arrived, remained a steadfast source of news.

Little discussion groups sprang up and slowly grew larger, frequented by students, lecturers, and ideologues alike. Soon they became social meeting points that attracted everyone with a desire to hear and debate the latest on the Gate, or with questions on more distant developments. Um Mabrouk's gathering place became the mouth of a river that filled the queue with news and rumors. Sometimes they were invented from within and shipped upstream, while other times the queue accepted rumors arriving from far-off places. Either way, they inevitably churned through Um Mabrouk's stand before being passed along.

Um Mabrouk soon put all her skills to use to invent a series of excuses and apologies to defend the woman with the short hair, and evade the threats from the man in the *galabeya*. He harassed her relentlessly now that the woman with the short hair had attracted an audience whose size rivaled—sometimes even exceeded—that of his own weekly lessons. Several times he advised Um Mabrouk to distance herself from the woman and to stop providing space for her meetings, and when she didn't obey him, he berated and shamed her, and ordered her to throw the woman out right away. But Um Mabrouk—who had raised nearly enough money for her daughter's treatment—was unshakable and faced him brazenly, refusing to get rid of her new friend. Encouraged by the people around her, she disobeyed him and got rid of her free phone, and bought a cheap one instead. When he realized how outright rebellious she was being, and that she was no longer under his control, he forbade her from attending his weekly lesson. Gathering for any purpose other than to pray and understand religion was hateful, he repeatedly announced; it caused people to lose God's favor, brought His wrath upon them, and was tantamount to apostasy.

But despite the best efforts of the woman with the short hair, a few months later the Violet Telecom boycott campaign waned. The issue was hard for people to fathom, especially as fewer and fewer citizens had been disappearing recently. Yet there remained a prevailing belief that a new wave of disappearances was yet to come, and people stayed on their guard. They left their phones in empty rooms at home, afraid that their important or revealing conversations would be transmitted, and kept their calls to short social pleasantries, congratulations, and condolences. No one was able to change phone networks to avoid such precautionary measures. Again and again other networks explained that they were completely subscribed and couldn't take on any more customers. Meanwhile, Violet Telecom continued to hold its lottery twice a month, and no one ever heard of someone who'd won a free phone declining it.

Under Um Mabrouk's protection, the woman with the short hair strengthened her popularity and defied a string of threats and countless fervent prayers from the man in the *galabeya*. He had singled her out in group prayers, claiming that the path she'd chosen led to an abyss of corruption, and that she was planting seeds of evil among people by urging them to think, and ask questions, and engage in other such undesirable activities. But she paid him no attention. Instead she developed a daily program: she would take all the flyers that Um Mabrouk collected, decide which news was the most important (anything to do with the Gate came first, of course), and then mark those in red for people who could read, and read them aloud to those who could not.

One day, in a departure from this routine, she spent the morning reading out corrections and clarifications in *The Truth*. Apparently, investigations had revealed that the foreigner previously accused of orchestrating the Disgraceful Events was a medical officer implicated in certain war crimes. He had fled his homeland years ago and reappeared here, changed his religion, married, and settled down under a new name in District 11. He'd stayed out of political activities and hostilities, despite what he'd done in his own country under a powerful regime that fell shortly after he left. The piece added that his embassy had released a statement stating that his country's judiciary had halted prosecution after confirming that he had died a natural death. After the judiciary's arms had searched for him for half a century, the man's case had been closed. This brief redaction took up just a few lines at the bottom of the second-to-last page, while the front page was plastered with a large headline about spies in the country and an article on the long history of unrest that they had stirred up while undercover.

The truth was clear for all to see, and Shalaby was thrown into confusion. His pride was broken, his shoulders sagged, and he didn't say another word about his story, though before that day he'd never tired of rehashing the details, which few people were actually interested in. At noon, he gathered his resolve and, despite their history, asked Ines to save his place for him. She immediately agreed, without asking any questions. In those brief hours, he seemed to have changed from his usual self, so much so that she pitied him. His voice had become hollow, his face was filled with weariness, even shame.

But she didn't delight in his sorrow as he had in hers. Shalaby, she'd discovered from people around them, was down on his luck; he and his family and his cousin's family desperately needed a steady income to escape the landowner's threats and intimidation. Yet she also knew that this wasn't the only reason he was waiting to process his paperwork at the Gate. He had once confessed to her that he deeply wished to bring his family a title that was worth something, something that would make them glorious and renowned in their poor little town, something to put them on a par with the landowner.

He had arrived an optimistic braggart and was now dejected and confused. He was uncertain of what to do, just as she was, and like her was overcome by a slew of calamities that had arrived one after the next. In her case, it was all thanks to her loose lips and a tongue she couldn't keep in check. She hadn't been like this before coming to the queue, not at all. Something frightening had come over her here, changing her; she never used to talk back to anyone or pick fights, and had never delved into others' affairs. Now she was the complete opposite. The strange thing was that after each slip of the tongue, she vowed she would go back to her usual self—quiet, introverted, and reserved—but then she would break her own promise the first chance she got. She was relieved to hear the correction in the newspaper; at least the person actually responsible for killing people during the Events had still not been identified. The matter had not yet been resolved, so what she'd said about Mahfouz and Shalaby and the other guards could still be proven right and beyond reproach. But she realized that there was no one to protect or defend her if disaster struck in the meantime. What friends did she have here in times of need, with this mouth of hers that would only get her into more trouble?

Later that afternoon, the woman with the short hair read out another piece from *The Truth* with a sarcastic smile. There was an unusual ad in the *Help Wanted* section about a new department in the Booth. It said anyone seeking employment there should submit their paperwork, including certificates and permits from their university and the Gate, and would undergo a personal interview within a week. It included an address where applications should be sent by registered mail:

The Gate's Booth, Communications Department, Behind the Restricted Zone. Nagy chuckled when he heard it, and told the woman that this was by far the strangest ad she'd read yet; there were no job summary, candidate profile, responsibilities, requirements, or conditions. Yet even so, it was an attractive government job with a steady salary and holiday allowance. He still hadn't heard back from the translation department; as usual, his checkered past kept him from being hired anywhere. He considered submitting an application to this new department, not because he thought he had a shot at the job but just to spite the hiring committee. They would certainly be surprised by his file and his nerve at applying for any job, much less this one. He waved at Ehab when he saw him approaching and told him about his idea, but Ehab surprised him by saying that he was going to submit an application, too. Ehab lowered his voice to say that he suspected the ad might be connected to the phone-tapping operation. They still didn't know the extent of the surveillance or how long it would continue, and they could get no information about those who'd vanished, although the disappearances were becoming less frequent.

Shalaby left the queue for a couple of hours and then returned without his leather bag or wristwatch, empty-handed except for a shiny golden medal on a dark-blue ribbon. He told everyone that he'd gotten it from the Booth in honor of his cousin Mahfouz. He'd shown the officials their mistake and they'd found his name on their lists, and he would be given a Certificate of Appreciation, just as soon as it was stamped by the Gate. Nagy recognized the medal, but he didn't want to expose Shalaby's fabrication and didn't say a word. He only laughed and laughed until tears rolled down his cheeks.

THE VISIT

In a surprising development, Amani called Nagy. For several weeks she hadn't seen or spoken to anyone but Yehya, who hobbled to the office when he was feeling well enough to spend an hour or two with her. At first Nagy didn't realize it was her; the number that appeared on his phone wasn't the one he had saved for her, and without giving him a chance to ask questions or even to say hello, she asked him to meet her immediately. At the corner by the coffee shop, across from the restaurant, she walked in circles on trembling legs, waiting for Nagy to appear. The doctor in uniform had visited her again.

He had come to her office a few days before and threatened her in front of her boss and colleagues. It hadn't been an explicit threat, but he'd said he was waiting for Yehya to pay him a visit at Zephyr Hospital. He'd said that Yehya had to have an operation, to avoid complications that could cause his health to rapidly decline, more rapidly than she could imagine . . . complications that could even be life-threatening. Before leaving her office, he'd turned and told her that he knew exactly where Yehya was. And if Yehya didn't show up at his office within the next few days, the man said, it might save him time to pay Yehya a visit himself.

When Nagy arrived she looked around wildly and pleaded with him to keep Yehya from visiting her, to keep him from coming to the office at all, or anywhere else, even to her apartment. The queue was safer, she thought; at least no one had disappeared there without returning, eventually. She still hadn't uttered a word about those terrible days, which had come rushing back to her at the sight of the doctor alone. Things had happened to her that no one else knew, things she couldn't speak of, things she still hadn't admitted even to herself.

She spoke so hurriedly that Nagy wasn't able to get a word in at first. He was shocked to see her so disturbed, and so he agreed to her request without question, and assured her that it would all work out and Yehya would be fine. Gripped with anxiety, she begged them to be careful, and he tried to calm her down. Maybe the doctor's words were just an empty threat; these people often relied on fear, scaring others to stop them from thinking straight or acting rationally. He kept talking to her in an attempt to reassure her, but she didn't hear a word he was saying. She just repeated herself in confusion, and then rushed away so quickly that she staggered and nearly fell several times, as Nagy watched her go.

He wandered around, thinking about what he should do now. His attempts to comfort Amani were just the first words that had come into his head and then out of his mouth, and he couldn't even believe them himself. Yehya wasn't well enough to run away, and he was too stubborn to consider it, much less be bullied into it. In the queue he was constantly surrounded by other people, and he seemed safe enough for now. But once or twice a week he went home to rest and regain some energy, energy he was losing day by day with the grueling effort of staying alive. Winter was looming and soon he wouldn't be able to stay in the queue day and night as people did now. Yehya's apartment was no secret, and neither was Nagy's. The neighbors knew them; neither place would be safe for him.

Nagy lost himself in all the complications, his head a torrent of disparate thoughts, and he realized that he'd arrived at the microbus stop without realizing it. He felt fatigue bearing down on him, so he squeezed himself into the first bus that arrived and decided to let himself be taken to wherever the line ended.

He yawned and rested his temple against the window, making circles of condensation with his dewy breath and doodling in them, an old favorite pastime. The streets were empty at this hour. Even all the cats and dogs had vanished, except for a single plump cat, also yawning, on top of a white car covered with a considerable layer of dirt. The sky was faintly lit; thick clouds veiled the rays of the sun, tempering the air, while dusk lay heavy on the horizon. It was the hour when particles of dust and debris seemed suspended in the emptiness, neither falling to earth nor disappearing into space.

The bus passed an arrow-shaped sign with PUBLIC ROAD written across it in thick letters. It pointed toward a steep ramp veering off to the right of the highway, and, unperturbed, Nagy realized that he was heading up a hill. They were going in the direction of the newspaper headquarters, and it occurred to him that he could try to catch Ehab, who'd raced off to the office with a new investigative report. But for now Nagy savored the sensation of letting his mind drift, and put his thoughts aside. Signs rolled by, one after another, until finally the driver announced the end of the line. He stopped the microbus beneath a giant sign with the phrase REMEMBER GOD written in thick white letters, above a cell number and signature: *Abbas*.

He wasn't far from the newspaper headquarters; he could see it just down the road, and he got off the bus leisurely and headed toward the unassuming building. He figured he should tell Ehab what he'd learned from Amani, but he wasn't convinced that it was worth seeking him out. Even with this information, what could either of them do? Inside, he inquired about Ehab, and another employee told him he was in a meeting with the editor in chief. Nagy left his name with her and went to wait outside. He sat down on the sidewalk across the street and leaned his head against an old tree trunk, feeling the branches drape themselves around him and the ancient scent of pine fall over him. Maybe it was time for Yehya to stop being so obstinate, even if he felt it was an insult to back down. The situation was dire, and he was no longer the only one implicated; Amani had been drawn into the game as well, which meant it would be hard for things between them to go back to how they were before.

In the years stretching between his studious university days and that afternoon, the two of them were all he knew, his closest friends, despite how different they all were. Amani and Yehya hadn't been drawn to each other out of an effortless, natural compatibility; they were both strong-willed and stubborn. Amani was headstrong, a trait he hadn't often seen in women, while Yehya's tenacity never abandoned him, and he never lost his faith in his ability to turn a situation to his favor. Yehya would never admit that he was just a single, powerless man in a society where rules and restrictions were stronger than everything else, stronger than the ruler himself, stronger than the Booth and even the Gate.

Nagy had failed to convince them that everything in the world was interconnected, and that their lives were ruled by a network of intricate and powerful relations. Even things that seemed random operated according to this invisible system, even if the connections couldn't be seen. Yehya laughed whenever they discussed it seriously, teasing him that the philosophy department had corrupted his mind and destroyed his faith in human nature. Amani would laugh, too—she could never be convinced that the independence she believed she possessed was in truth no more than an accepted illusion, part of a web of relations and contradictions. The Gate itself was an integral part of the system, too, even if from the outside it appeared to pull all the strings.

One day long ago, he'd told Amani that everything she did, even if seemingly trivial and irrelevant, had reverberations in the grand scheme of things. Even something apparently insignificant—like the amount of air she breathed—could have consequences. He had smiled to himself while assuming an outward solemnity, and added that, for example, the meager rent she paid her landlord could have contributed to the Gate's sudden appearance in the heart of the city. And conversely, he told her, she was affected by everything that happened, too, even if she didn't admit it; if the Gate announced a ban on kites with colored streamers, it could indirectly influence her daily life or work. This interrelation was real, even if there were no explicit connections. At the time, she'd laughed and told him he was completely mad.

For as long as he'd known her, she'd never cared for politics or philosophy. No matter what happened, she focused only on the concrete details of everyday life. Yehya was just like her: he would rather deal with tangible reality and the things he knew firsthand. And so Nagy was always the odd one out, the one who paid little attention to life's minor details and often appeared lost amid it all. He saw only the wider context, the systems that everything was governed by. He wasn't interested in the little pieces; he wanted to understand the broader picture, how it worked and what it meant. At first he'd envied their safe, secure lives, while he had been battered by the Gate's tempestuous wrath; but now he was going to lose Yehya, and Amani, too. He would be left alone, powerless and bound to life as it had become, no longer capable of the liberty he'd once enjoyed. If he were still a student, or even a hopeful young lecturer, he would change everything about the queue, defend his friends fearlessly, and persist until he'd brought down the Gate and the whole system with it.

He was roused from his reveries by a friendly smack on the shoulder from Ehab.

"Hey, Nagy, I wasn't expecting you."

"I just happened to stop by—you won't believe what happened this morning."

"Let's talk on the way. You're going to the queue, too, right? Listen, my boss doesn't want to publish any more reports about the queue. He refused the article I wrote a week ago, and today he turned down another one, and before these two he took everything important out of an article I'd written about my trip to Zephyr Hospital with Amani. Can you believe it, he cut three whole paragraphs down to two and a half lines; it looked like a greeting card when he was done with it! And he even rejected my piece on the Violet Telecom boycott. He threw it down on his desk when he saw the headline, and then refused to give it back to me when I asked him for it. I'm telling you, that man is suspicious, acting all high and mighty—how can he ban an article on the phone-company scandal while allowing an article that attacked Zephyr Hospital, even if it *was* short and more vague?"

THE NEWSPAPER

The Truth increased its distribution and ran an intriguing interview with the High Sheikh. A bold subtitle hinted that the interview occurred partly in response to rumors that innocent citizens had been shot down by gunfire during the first and second Disgraceful Events, the very notion of which was questionable at best. The rumors were outrageous, it said; unconscionable accusations. In a special column outlined with a thick border, it noted that the Gate had denied these fabrications repeatedly, but to no avail, as they had only spread further.

The editor in chief wrote a brief introduction, in which he explained that His Eminence the High Sheikh, who headed the Fatwa and Rationalizations Committee, had recently received questions from believers about the amendment to Article 4 (A) and related rumors. He had issued a fatwa in response, which, the editor said, was met with overwhelming gratitude from the general public. He also emphasized that His Eminence was the sole person able to illuminate the way forward in these trying times, in which the wise and ignorant alike weighed in with their own opinions. The Sheikh's explanation in the interview was so comforting that, as was noted in the article, the interviewer had to stop the recording several times to express his deep gratitude and admiration.

The Sheikh told the interviewer that the fatwa contained

two separate decrees, one for each of two categories of people. The first was for those who had started and spread the rumors: he deemed them liars and hypocrites. But the fatwa was primarily dedicated to the second category: believers who were weak of faith. The matter there, he said, was simple and clear. He began by confirming that piety protects people from misfortune and evil—religious scholars and ordinary citizens all knew this to be true. Therefore, if citizens were pious, God-fearing believers (and not weak of faith), they would not bring destruction upon themselves. On the contrary, he said, they would instinctively avoid suspicious people and questionable or forbidden places.

Assertions that people had been injured in the Events were clearly no more than lies and fabrications, spread by an anti-religious minority who had suffered injuries themselves. Most people in the nation were believers (thank God!) and so he had no reason to fear for them, not even in the face of bullets. Yet even believers should take precautions to ensure that God keeps them from harm, he added—precautions such as dedicating one's life to reciting prayers, for example.

The High Sheikh invoked a few passages from the Greater Book, explaining that if a believer were to be struck by a bullet (despite his prayers and supplication), his faith would guide him to the understanding that it was *God himself* who'd struck him down. A wounded believer should not despair or oppose God's will. Nor should he question the unquestionable—such an act could lead him down a perilous path toward doubt. Instead, the believer must accept the will of God. He must acknowledge how lucky he was to be struck by a bullet, and exalted to a place in heaven ordinarily reserved only for the most dutiful.

At the end of the interview, the High Sheikh noted that everything he had said was part of the fatwa. The Fatwa and Rationalizations Committee had ratified it definitively in its last meeting, and it would be announced at a big press conference within days, to help reassure citizens who were suffering from confusion.

A large photograph of the High Sheikh was printed in the center of the page, him with his solemn smile and the interviewer sitting in front of him. In conclusion, the article stated that the Sheikh commended the newspaper's efforts to uphold the word of truth, which was why he had given them an exclusive interview.

Yehya sat in front of Um Mabrouk on a plastic chair, his leg resting on the stone table. He had a cup of tea in one hand and the report that Ehab had written—a different copy of the same report that the editor in chief had ripped up—in the other. Ehab sat beside him, next to him was Nagy, and strewn around them on the ground was a mess of newspapers. Yehya shrugged and said that the editor in chief had made the right call: the report wasn't fit to print. The story simply made no sense—it contradicted all the other accounts in all the other papers, as well as every statement released by the Gate, and it went against the Committee's latest fatwas, too. Ehab's report was just based on rumors: rumors that there were citizens injured by government bullets who hadn't come forward, and that others were blind to their injuries. Rumors that they had disposed of the bullets removed from people's bodies, and then denied that the bullets had ever existed. Rumors that a few people had managed to climb over the stone barricades, enter the Restricted Zone, and approach the Northern Building. Rumors that some of them had been killed by birdshot, but that the survivors had rallied and retreated, only to disappear completely. Rumors that they had not been seen since.

Ehab had also included a short paragraph about the microbus driver who had reported seeing an injured young man carrying a bag of spent birdshot covered in blood, during the second Disgraceful Events. Ehab noted that after this testimony was made public, the driver had disappeared. Then the Gate had announced that the driver was a well-known, long-term drug user, addicted to hallucinogens. The young man he spoke of didn't exist, the Gate's statement said, and neither did his injured leg, as no trace had been found of either. Ehab quoted an article stating that the driver had been admitted to a government clinic to treat his addiction, but that no one knew where he was being treated or whether he'd been released. Yehya handed the papers back to Ehab with a snort of derisive laughter, while Nagy shifted in his seat and told him that he should make copies to distribute in the queue.

People passed hearsay, a growing number of leaflets, and newspaper articles along the queue; they feverishly searched for fresh information anywhere and any way they could, while time passed and no one moved an inch forward. Most recently, a postal worker joined the queue, carrying an official petition addressed to the Gate from a group of people called the "Disgraceful Events Victims Association." It openly accused the High Sheikh of causing distress across the nation because he had questioned the faith of the injured in his interview in *The Truth*.

The petition's signatories said that the interview had damaged their reputations among their families, acquaintances, and colleagues, and they attached certified documents proving that they were devout believers. Many held Certificates of True Citizenship, and moreover, they really were injured. Their petition included legal grounds, prepared by a lawyer who was also gravely wounded. It proved that the fatwa was riddled with errors, and they demanded that it be repealed and reviewed before being made public.

In response, the Center for Freedom and Righteousness delivered its own urgent petition to the Booth. Based on the High Sheikh's interview, it accused the injured of failing to perform their obligatory religious duties, and stated that this negligence had directly caused their injuries. The Center demanded that these people's files be handed over to the Fatwa and Rationalizations Committee in full, so that it could rule on their cases and take appropriate measures against them. Yet despite the general outrage, the fatwa wasn't revoked or even amended. It had already been announced in a press conference, and a series of supporting statements was released in the days that followed, while the latest message from the Gate denied that anything called the Restricted Zone had ever existed.

THE LESSON

The man in the *galabeya* rose to the occasion and began his thirty-first weekly lesson in support of the High Sheikh's fatwa. In his opening remarks, he said that the fatwa represented the esteemed Committee, which included religious scholars of purest intention and infallible opinion. He added that to question them or gossip about matters of religion—as some fools were doing—was religiously impermissible.

He and his followers had arranged rows of chairs at the front of the queue to accommodate the growing number of listeners. After a prolonged debate over proper religious seating arrangements, the first row was designated for the women, so that they wouldn't be harassed if they stood at the back. Ines sat front and center and listened with rapt attention. She wore a drab *isdal* over her everyday clothes, and it fell from the middle of her forehead down to her toes, so that every hill and valley of her body was concealed. After concluding the lesson and answering all questions, the man in the *galabeya* looked closely at the women and then launched into a prayer praising these modestly dressed believers who followed the path of righteousness, emphasizing what good wives and mothers they were.

He arose from his seat to distribute an array of small booklets to the women, with titles like *The Nature of Women, Torment and Blessing in the Grave, Suffering the Temptation of*

Women, and *Conjugal Rights*. He gave Ines the whole collection, saying it was a small gift to welcome her into a sisterhood of repentance and to celebrate her return to the path of guidance and truth. The booklets would help her learn more about faith, the world, and religious practicalities.

He returned to his seat and spoke of the importance of the High Sheikh's fatwa. It not only set matters straight, but also lifted people out of their ignorance and confusion by educating them on the vile conspiracies being hatched against the nation. He thanked and praised various centers and associations, all led by hardworking, God-fearing men, who had taken it upon themselves to lead the charge of societal reform down a path of righteousness. He concluded by declaring his solidarity with the Center for Freedom and Righteousness, and announced that he was a signatory of its most recent petition, which proposed that the intentions of the injured, and their religious and ethical commitment, needed to be monitored.

Yehya grew angry as he listened to Ehab describe the fatwa and the week's lesson. He'd seen a change come over several people standing near him in the queue, even Ines, but he still wasn't keen on Nagy's suggestion to form an oppositional group, something like "The Honorable Injured Citizens Association," or "The Righteous and Injured." His mind was filled with a growing pain that painkillers could no longer alleviate, and the medicine itself knocked him out. It made him dizzy and unable to focus, so much so that he couldn't even check in on Amani.

Ines hadn't missed a single weekly lesson since committing herself to her new attire. She felt a deep sense of relief and was gradually accepted by a new crowd, which was somewhat different from the groups of women she'd known at her school.

She joined them for social and spiritual activities, visited proselytizers, and attended religious gatherings and prayer groups. Most meetings were held outside the queue, and the women would gather in a clique and head to a designated car, which dropped them at the meeting place and returned them to the queue when it was over. She became immersed in it all and her fears began to fade, though she was still occasionally troubled by worrisome thoughts. Attending meetings meant she spent less time in the queue, and while she was no longer concerned about Shalaby, she had developed an interest in Yehya.

Meanwhile, the man in the *galabeya* channeled his efforts in two directions. He opened a small center near the queue to help people who wanted to obtain a Certificate of True Citizenship from the Gate. He had discovered that this was all that many people were waiting for, and he was sure that most of them would fail to meet the criteria. He also began to collect donations in support of Violet Telecom, which he regularly lauded during his lessons, as the company had declared its commitment to developing new services for its customers who could not afford them.

He asked Ines to help him reach as many women in the queue as she could, especially those who didn't regularly attend his weekly lessons. She agreed right away and began working alongside him. They didn't get off to a good start. Ehab and Yehya started an argument with the man in the *galabeya*, and they were quickly joined by Nagy, and the four of them exchanged a fierce barrage of insults. Ehab accused him of being financially corrupt, and he accused them of being morally bankrupt, hinting that the Center for Freedom and Righteousness' petition applied to Yehya because of the injury that he was attempting to hide. It would likely lead him to be questioned before the Fatwa and Rationalizations Committee, convicted unanimously as an Untrue Citizen, and duly punished. The fight ended before either side had achieved a definitive victory, and no one had been physically harmed, but Ines was distraught. Yehya had been at the top of her list of people to approach for donations. Her situation felt so precarious, especially without someone to lean on, and Yehya seemed like a good man, perhaps even a decent marriage prospect. She knew he didn't have a cell phone and hadn't joined the Violet Telecom boycott, nor did he seem interested in doing so. Fundraising had seemed like a perfect way to get to know him.

She'd been successful in soliciting donations from the new arrivals, women who had just joined the queue and were ignorant of the phone-tapping scandal. She managed to convince two women to promise that they would attend lessons, and had collected a moderate amount of money from a few of the wealthier people. The man in the *galabeya* told her how impressed he was by her cleverness, and on the day of prayer he asked for her hand in marriage. She pretended to be flustered and surprised, and demurely looked down at the ground, as she'd always imagined she would do in such a situation, and then asked if he would allow her some time to consult her family. She left the queue the next day and went to her sister's, having realized that she was too unsettled to spend the night alone in her big apartment. She stayed for days, but despite all their conversations she couldn't reach a decision. Her sister wasn't enthusiastic and didn't encourage her to accept his proposal. From the way Ines had described him, the man didn't seem like a good match for her at all.

Ines kept silent about the trouble she was in; she didn't want to be scolded and didn't want to frighten her sister, or deal with the consequences if she did. She called her mother and father to ask for advice, and discovered that they were more accepting than she had expected. She asked God for guidance and realized that she was comfortable with the idea of someone beside her, able to share her burdens, who she could lean on in times of need. The time she spent in her sister's house further convinced her; her brother-in-law was clearly annoyed by having another person in their space, and she realized that she wouldn't be able to stay there if she found herself in trouble.

As life in the queue went on, Amani's life gradually broke down. She stopped going to work regularly, but her boss didn't reprimand her or even ask why. One day he walked into her office and told her to type up a request for leave without pay. He told her to hand over all her customers' telephone numbers to another employee, and was so keen to have her gone that he didn't even check on whether she'd returned the office supplies, as was customary. She looked out the window, and in her reflection she saw two dark circles in place of her eyes. She slept only in scarce, sporadic spells, waking up terrified in the middle of the night, lying there for long minutes in the darkness, unable to see, her eyelids so heavy that she could not open her eyes.

SIX

Document No. 6

Follow-Up

Information contained in this file has been regularly updated, and individuals responsible for observation and the collection of information are kindly asked to ensure its veracity before transmitting it to the record-keeper. The contents of this document shall not be disclosed under any condition without official signed and stamped permission. Inquiring as to the identity of the individuals tasked with updating this information is not permitted.

Notes

This document examines the patient's status after he left the hospital and was no longer under close medical supervision. It aims to create a comprehensive picture of the environment and conditions in which the patient lives and operates, to monitor possible developments (both medical and non-medical), and observe his close friends and acquaintances. Only doctors attending to this case and those with designated official IDs are permitted to examine this file, regardless of their professional specialization.

The document contained more information than it had when Tarek had first begun to examine Yehya's file. It included a detailed description of his movements, a chart of his acquaintances and friends, and maps of places he frequented. The introduction alone was practically an entire report in itself, which covered his whole life history, from his birth to when he first attended school and up to his work at the company. Tarek examined the document fervently, realizing that he was remarkably similar to Yehya in many regards. An only child born to a middle-class family, with a father who worked in the public sector and a mother who stayed at home; they had both gone to private elementary school, then transferred to public school because of rising tuition fees, and uneventfully graduated from high school with good grades.

Yehya had occasionally played in a small sports club during those days, though without remarkable success except in volleyball, where the coach had named him a star player, but he quit the team when he entered university. The document stated that Yehya hadn't been involved in any political activity during his studies in the commerce department. But Tarek didn't understand how that could be true, since it also said that Yehya had often been seen in the company of several unruly and rebellious students. Yehya joined a theater group at university, just as Tarek had done during his own studies. Yehya published several attempts at poetry in university journals, which is how he met his girlfriend, Amani Sayed Ibra him, who was covered extensively in the following paragraph. He graduated with decent grades, completed his service in the Deterrence Force, and then worked as a sales representative for a reputable company in District 4. The company sold cleaning products, and Yehya lived by himself in a small apartment near his family in District 9. He'd never gone to the Gate or the Booth for a permit or certificate before, and there was no Certificate of True Citizenship in his Personnel File. At the end of the paragraph was a note that made Tarek pause every time:

> The owner of the company was informed that his employees' Personnel Files were incomplete; he was instructed that all Personnel Files must include a Certificate of True Citizenship.

Did the lack of a Certificate imply that Yehya had never engaged in any oppositional activities, and therefore hadn't been required to obtain one? Or, was it the reverse—did it mean that Yehya really was a dissident, and thus was denied the Certificate when he needed it? No matter how many times he'd reread the file, Tarek still didn't know what to make of this line. Perhaps, he thought now, the Certificate-granting department had somehow overlooked Yehya's activities or his file, despite its apparent omnipotence. After all, things like that sometimes happened at the hospital.

The chart of friends and acquaintances was followed by two large paragraphs and a third shorter one. The first was about Amani Sayed Ibrahim. Thirty-seven years old, she was unmarried and lived in District 6 by herself. Her father had died several years earlier, and her brothers lived in the out-lying districts. She graduated from law school with honors and appeared to have met Yehya during her time at university. They had grown closer during those years, and worked at the same company after graduation; she took a position in the telephone sales department and had never put her law degree to use. Tarek learned from the report that she was in constant contact with Yehya, she accompanied him nearly everywhere except to the Gate. He also read that she was a prime factor in his stubbornness about the bullet; she supported his decision to stand in the queue and prevented him from undergoing surgery. She had never submitted an application for a permit or certificate from the Gate, either.

The second paragraph concerned an individual named Nagy Saad. It said that he was the patient's closest friend; they'd been in the same class in school. He'd graduated with a philosophy degree, second in his class, and was a former university lecturer, though currently unemployed. Tarek figured that this was the man who'd come to the hospital with Yehya and Amani but didn't join them in his office. The paragraph mentioned that he had been detained by the Deterrence Force during his second year at university, due to acts in violation of the university social order, in which he had helped to write instigative pamphlets and distribute them to other students.

His appointment as a lecturer in the philosophy department was approved so that he could remain under the security forces' supervision, and he persisted with his actions in violation of the educational process, before resigning as a result of his inappropriate and aberrant ideas. The students complained about them, and he was frequently advised to keep himself in line. When the dean of the university told him he needed to supply a Certificate of True Citizenship, he'd arrived with a resignation letter instead and thrown it in the man's face. The dean had later submitted a complaint to the Booth accusing Nagy of contempt for him and for the Gate. Nagy was detained a second time, in the home of the patient, Yehya Gad el-Rab Saeed, for possession of offensive papers that he was on his way to distribute. This time he confessed to the crime. He claimed that Yehya was unaware of his intentions, that he'd only coincidentally stopped by Yehya's house, and was released shortly afterward. But his request for a Certificate of True Citizenship was refused by the Gate when he applied for a job at a news agency. Tarek learned that Nagy rarely left Yehya's side; unemployed and unable to find another job, he seemed to spend nearly all his time with him.

The third paragraph was about Ehab, but it didn't contain much information. The reader was referred to another file, a much older one in the basement under the name "Ehab Ahmed Salem," and the reference number was clearly specified. The only significant detail in the paragraph was that Ehab had recently sent his paperwork to the Booth, in application for a job advertised by the communications department.

The next paragraph included a detailed description of Yehya's movements from the moment he fled Zephyr Hospital to the day he had arrived at the queue. It seemed he'd been given special attention; the observer missed nothing, even details that seemed inconsequential. It stated that he went to Amani's house the day he turned thirty-nine, and one of the paragraphs included a brief note, also mentioned in the introduction, about the letter she had sent him in the queue via Um Mabrouk. Yehya's brief encounter with an eye doctor was mentioned in passing, too. She had advised him to go to the Booth to get a Certificate of True Citizenship, which was necessary in order to obtain a permit. They walked there together, because she needed the official's approval on an eye exam that her sister had undergone before the Gate would accept it.

Tarek found these last few lines confusing, and he asked a colleague about protocol for eye examinations. He was told that vision tests needed to be approved by the Booth, and that five percent of the results were determined by the official. He usually added the full five percent to the patient's score, unless he happened to be annoyed that day. Yehya's meetings with Mrs. Alfat, the head nurse, were observed and recorded in detail, especially their second meeting. It said that Yehya had asked her about her work at the hospital, and whether each nurse had her own specialization. He appeared to be satisfied by her answers, and then he asked her straight out if she would help him remove the bullet, and offered her a considerable sum of money if she would do the surgery herself. He said he would pay her as soon as it was finished, as long as she gave him the bullet. The following sentence said that he showed her a booklet of legal statements exempting her from criminal and medical liability, leaving all responsibility with him if he came to any harm. After Yehya's offer there was a blank space on the page, and Tarek guessed it was reserved for Mrs. Alfat's response. Nothing in the paragraph indicated whether she had accepted or rejected his offer.

He thought about it all, suddenly surprised, as if he were discovering it for the first time. He'd opened the file dozens of times, and had never let it out of his sight for long, but he still didn't have the slightest idea who was recording this information. The strangest part was that until now, Tarek had never truly wondered exactly who was updating the file, or how. He'd spent months among the pages, and every day there was an addition. Whoever it was, they updated it so meticulously, monitoring everything day after day, with dates and sometimes even times. Perhaps deep within himself, he was content watching Yehya from afar, somehow grateful for it all, afraid that if he dug too deep the writing would cease.

In addition to everything else in Document No. 6, Yehya's medical condition was also documented, and reading it, Tarek realized that Yehya's health was slowly deteriorating. There was no chance that his condition would stabilize, as he'd hoped it might. Yehya was urinating less frequently, only passing a few drops of liquid each time, which were pinkish and purulent. He often purchased large quantities of heavy-duty painkillers from nearby pharmacies, and his ability to walk and sit had clearly declined. Tarek nearly dropped the file in alarm when he read Yehya's latest symptoms. He stood up and called Amani, desperately hoping that they weren't true and that she would say something to assuage his guilt. But Amani didn't pick up. Maybe she was ignoring him because he'd abandoned them, or it was possible that something had happened to her. He felt as if his own mental state was declining, too; he turned the details over in his mind in their full absurdity, unable to disentangle them from his own emotions. If only he'd just done the surgery before he'd found out that he needed a permit. Even if they had investigated him and summoned him to the Gate, he might have looked like an ignorant fool, swearing he hadn't known about the law, but he wouldn't have been forced to lie. Yet now he did know: he couldn't pretend otherwise, and couldn't bring himself to lie.

Annex 1

Individuals Accompanying the Patient

	Age	*ID No:*
1. *Amani Sayed Ibrahim*	37	0307011602131
2. *Ismail Mohamed Abdullah*	—	—
3. *Ragi Sherif Saad*	—	—
4. *Mariam Fouad Selim*	—	—
5. *Maged Ahmed Fathy*	—	—

The last document in the file contained the names of people who carried Yehya to the nearest hospital when he was shot. Tarek did not recognize any of them except for Amani's, which was at the top of the list. There were names of four others, three men and a woman, but no information about who they were. There weren't even ID numbers, and they didn't appear in the chart of friends and acquaintances, which accounted for most of the file. There was no one he could call to lead him to Yehya, and so he couldn't offer any help, even though he knew how much Yehya was suffering. Yet he was unable to ignore it all, either, or to pretend as if none of it had happened. The constant turmoil, and his own helplessness in controlling his thoughts and feelings, were choking him. He had been suspended in this gray area, doing nothing for months since he had first opened the file. Now, suddenly, in a moment of wild rage, he decided to go to the queue in search of Yehya.

He arrived at nightfall. The air had a cold bite to it, sending shivers through his whole body, and there wasn't enough light to make out people's faces. It was impossible to search through the crowds one by one; a few people offered to guide him, but he had no answer for the question they each asked: "Where in the queue did he say he was?" He'd heard so much about this place, and had listened with intrigue to the stories that new doctors and nurses exchanged, but he'd never imagined that he would find himself lost among its crowds. He'd never imagined that he would fail to find the man whose body bore an injury that set him apart from everyone else, and whose face never left Tarek's mind, not even while he slept.

He walked as far as he could toward the front, but he never arrived there. Each time he identified a gathering of people in the dim light and imagined he was finally at the head of the queue, he realized that it was just another stop, something like a rest stop. He gradually began to realize how vast the queue was, and what the driver had meant when he told passengers, "This bus goes to the end of the queue, just to the box; if you want the head of the queue, take the other bus."

Yehya wasn't there, or if he was, Tarek couldn't find him. Lights went out and people began to settle down for the night, while others left to return in the morning, but Yehya didn't appear among those sleeping or leaving. Tarek took out his phone and tried to call Amani again, but she didn't pick up this time, either, as if she, too, had vanished. He felt an overwhelming sense of loneliness; he was a stranger here. There was a cold sweat on his forehead, his stomach tightened, and he was seized by a single thought: a desire to return to where he had come from, that warm and well-lit room. He found himself in a microbus, automatically getting off in front of the hospital. Once there, he locked the door to his office behind him, swallowed several sedatives, and sat there alone and lost in thought, Yehya's file open before him.

THE NIGHTMARE

For weeks before she'd left her job, Amani hadn't made any sales; she would call her usual customers and then lose her temper in the middle of the conversation by picking needless fights with them. When she hung up on one of their big clients, a hotel owner, her boss called her into his office, took a sizable cut from her salary, and threatened to fire her.

She didn't object when two weeks later he told her to submit a request for leave without pay, but even after that things didn't improve. She never left the house, and walked around in a haze all day and night. She was unnerved, anxiously awaiting something indefinable. She was wary when opening the door to anyone, even the mailman, and whenever the Gate's announcements came onto the television she left the room.

She had nothing to do or think about, just her failure to get the X-ray. She blamed herself constantly, her thoughts spinning endlessly in circles as she thought about what she should have done, and all the mistakes she'd made in Zephyr Hospital. If it weren't for her, they would have succeeded, and Yehya would have had the surgery without a hitch.

One night when she couldn't sleep, she noticed several missed calls from Tarek on her phone. She thought about calling him back, but just the sight of his number terrified her. She imagined him telling her what tragedies awaited her, and her finger pressed the red button as if of its own volition, turning off the phone. She lay in bed, tossing and turning, her head spinning with images again. She imagined Yehya beside her, she felt him breathing and the way he smelled, and then closed her eyes and saw a bewildering entanglement. The memory of Um Mabrouk's daughter's funeral blended with an image of Yehya standing in a cemetery, wearing a gravedigger's uniform, and then he collapsed from loss of blood, dead.

Tarek visited her fitful dreams, too. He was looking at a bullet protruding from Yehya's stomach, but he didn't reach over to pluck it out. She saw Yehya entering the Gate and emerging on the other side, his body divided into horizontal strips, but the one with the bullet wasn't there. Meanwhile, Nagy repeated that the bullet was part of an integral whole that should never be divided, per hallowed philosophical and sociological theories: one must deal with it in its natural state, from which it should not be removed, so as to not disturb the context. In a corner of her dream was a huge and terrifying bulldozer digging a deep grave for Yehya to be buried in, and a man standing beside it; his face was cruel and familiar, but she couldn't tell exactly who he was.

Then the scene changed and she saw herself somewhere lavish and opulent; there were rich wood paneling, luxurious furniture, and supple carpets soft to the touch, but she didn't dare tread upon them, her feet looked so wretched against everything else. There was a black sign emblazoned with the words DEPARTMENT OF CONSPIRACIES in brilliant golden letters; she was the only one there. Then she was back in the graveyard, and this time she walking through it in utter darkness, passing others moving around as she was, in silence. The basement: intuitively she knew she was in the basement, as if the word had been suspended in the air the whole time. She didn't see it, but taking the situation in with all her senses, she had a terrifying moment of realization. And when she knew she was imprisoned there forever she awoke in a panic, the hair on her forearms alert and trembling, her tongue stuck in her parched throat. The nightmares repeated in myriad variations throughout the night, until she no longer knew the difference between dreams and reality.

WINTER

Winter had officially begun. So declared the message broadcast on television after the Gate's daily announcement, and the sun that had divided Yehya's body in two each noontime responded by slightly subsiding. There was a mild breeze, and he no longer needed to switch places with Nagy for the shade, but as the temperatures dropped, the throbbing and spasms in his left side grew stronger, until he moaned each time his chest filled and emptied of air. His urine was almost entirely blood now, and he could not bend at his knees or waist, so he spent all his time standing or stretched out on the sidewalk alongside the queue. He was rarely able to visit Um Mabrouk's gathering place these days, and Nagy never left his side.

Ehab dropped by at the usual time, on his way back from the Booth, where he'd just learned the results of the interview he'd done a while back for the position in the communications department. He passed the middle section of the queue on his way, collecting some news, and discovered that Ines had left for good. Apparently, she'd married the man in the *galabeya*. Before she departed, she'd given everything she'd carried with her those past few months to the Southern woman's son, telling him to give his mother her regards. Mabrouk had graduated from elementary school, even though he'd missed several exams while in the queue, and his kidney attacks had returned. Um Mabrouk had expanded her little shop, and on the advice of the woman with the short hair she'd bought a few clay pots and planted fresh mint. Finally he told them that the screening committee had rejected most applicants for the job, claiming that they all lacked practical experience and adequate skills. He had been the first to be turned down.

Yehya was worried about other things and didn't comment on Ehab's news until he'd finished. Then he asked if there was any word from Amani, but Ehab said no. Nagy decided to call her, and chose just the right moment, rescuing her from a well of confusion and indecision. Terrified, she told him about the barrage of calls she hadn't answered, and he gave the phone to Yehya. He spoke to her for less than a minute, but her words faltered while the din of the queue nearly drowned out Yehya's feeble voice, and they were barely able to hold a conversation.

Tarek's attempts to reach her caused them unforeseen anxiety, sending them into a discussion of all possible explanations. Maybe he'd decided to give them the X-ray, maybe he was thinking about doing the operation, maybe he, too, had been threatened, or had received an order to do it from deep within the depths of Zephyr Hospital. Whatever his intentions, they had to speak to him.

When Tarek arrived at the queue for a second time, preoccupied and withdrawn, he was easily able to find them because Nagy had described their location to him at length over the phone. He walked with Nagy to where Yehya sat on the ground, reading the newspapers that were scattered around him. Steam ascended from a cup, filled to the brim with hot tea, that he had placed by his left side, and Tarek was filled with shame when he saw it, knowing that Yehya was trying to ease his pain by keeping the area warm. He bent down to shake Yehya's hand, and sat beside him on the ground. They cordially exchanged a bit of small talk, tacitly agreeing not to delve into the details of the predicament.

Tarek admitted to himself that he had wanted to visit Yehya not only to confirm what he'd read in the file, but also to reassure himself. But seeing Yehya in person was different. His health truly was bad, worse than he'd read and worse than he'd expected. And there was nothing Tarek could do, nothing more than Yehya himself had done with the help of his friends.

THE BOOTH

Torrential rains poured down across the districts, flooding acres of land, including the plot that Shalaby and Mahfouz's families farmed. Their huts disintegrated, swept away in a downpour that didn't let up for days. Shalaby hurried home, making sure to take the medallion with him, and saw the ruin with his own eyes. The whole crop was destroyed, and the television and shower were gone, as were all of Mahfouz's clothes. There was nothing but water, nearly up to his knees. Shaken by the wails of his mother, aunt, and five younger sisters, he realized that the best solution was to visit the Booth again.

He took proof of the damage with him and asked for a new plot of land for the families, far from the crushing rain, but the official sitting in the Booth accused him of trying to swindle him, and having caused the downpour in the first place. Shalaby had deliberately flooded the huts, he said with confidence, to acquire land he could build a house on, instead of the soggy farmland where they could only build these flimsy shacks.

Shalaby froze for a moment, waiting for the official to finish his joke, but the man was completely serious. He'd been through so much in recent weeks; ridiculed and insulted, his honor and dignity dragged through the mud. His commander and unit had abandoned him, as had the Gate; he'd even been forced to lie to people just to save face, and this was the final indignity. Shalaby trembled with rage and grabbed the official by the throat with a roar, so suddenly that the man didn't have a chance step back. Shalaby sent his rough fist between the iron bars, landing a blow to the official's face, and then snatched the medallion from his shirt pocket and bashed his head with it before the people waiting behind him dragged him away in horror. Shalaby cursed and screamed that he was the cousin of a martyr, he had rights, the Gate owed it to him, and he would die like his cousin before abandoning his rights.

The story reached the entire queue within hours, people passed it around with a mixture of astonishment and delight, and the woman with the short hair announced it at her daily gathering. Some people expected that Shalaby would become the first person from the queue to be disappeared, but he returned a few days later. He was calmer, and insisted that he would stand in his place until the Gate opened, ignoring the questions that assailed him. A few days later, he confided in Um Mabrouk that he wanted to know the truth, but what truth that was exactly, he wouldn't say.

As the queue swelled and extended into far-off, practically uninhabited districts, the Gate issued a decree for a wall to be built around everyone waiting. For their own protection, of course. This was especially important, given evidence that had emerged of people trying to take advantage of the situation; certain individuals were attempting to meddle with security, tranquillity, and righteous citizens' minds. Not long after that, the people in the middle of the queue noticed that a man had appeared on the roof of the Northern Building, behind some kind of object on a tripod. It looked like a telescope, or an old film camera, and its barrel was aimed at the end of the queue. From the moment he appeared the man never abandoned his post, or at least no one ever saw him stand up or leave, not any time of day. When a few veterans of the queue decided to take shifts and observe him, they confirmed uneasily that after six solid days, he hadn't moved at all.

They had told her, before she was moved to the great nothingness, that nothing had happened, no injuries, no bullets, no files, nothing . . . but Amani hadn't believed it. Even so, perhaps their claims were true. She considered this as she listened to the Gate's breaking message, broadcast on the Youth Station, that a big-budget blockbuster had been filmed in the square recently. The countries involved in this joint production wanted it to look as natural as possible, so they kept the cameras and filming equipment hidden from view. The announcement added that it was one of the biggest action films in world history, explaining that this was why a few citizens had believed that there were bullets, tear gas, and smoke, even though there clearly hadn't been anything like that, nothing except for standard special effects. The Gate called on everyone to remain calm, and avoid being misled by rumors that had been invented and spread by deranged lunatics. It explained that life was to go on as usual.

Amani relaxed. She'd found what she'd long hoped for in the Gate's message—stability and tranquillity—while Yehya kept slowly bleeding. It was all a simple fiction, she decided; that was the rational and convincing explanation, but it had fooled her and everyone else. If only she'd accepted it from the start, she wouldn't have left her job, locked herself in the house, or withdrawn from the world. Yehya wouldn't have been in torment this whole time, imagining that he'd been implicated in a dangerous situation, or that he had a responsibility he couldn't ignore. She missed him so much, and Nagy, too, even Ehab, who she'd only seen once; she longed to see them all. Yes, nothing had really happened.

She surrendered to the conclusions that she began to weave around the Gate's message, driving dread, threats, and uncertainty to a dark corner of her mind, and banishing everything that robbed her of sleep. She felt liberated; freed from the fears that had wrapped around her life and mind for what felt like an eternity.

A weight had finally lifted from her chest. She opened her lungs and took a big gulp of air, and picked up her phone to call Nagy. She was unconcerned with his warnings, she had good news. Then she tried to convince Yehya that the bullet that had pierced his side and lodged itself in his pelvis was a fake bullet, that it wasn't important to remove it, and that he no longer needed to trouble himself with the matter of who had shot him. But Yehya was not convinced, and he did not stop bleeding.

TAREK'S PROPOSAL

Tarek heard the Gate's latest message and came to a decision: he would do the surgery. The Gate's assertions were becoming more outrageous by the day, and he knew that Yehya would die soon if nothing changed. He felt he had nothing to lose from one last-ditch attempt. He'd come up with an idea that was certainly unorthodox, but he was also convinced that it was sound. If he could operate on Yehya at one of his friends' houses, the home of Nagy or Amani perhaps, they could find a way around the permit. The laws issued by the Gate only applied to hospitals and clinics, and said nothing about ordinary people in their homes. Tarek could bring the surgical instruments he needed with him and perform the operation there. It would be easiest if Alfat accepted Yehya's offer and agreed to help them, and maybe he could show them how to remove the bullet without he himself having to lay a finger on Yehya at all.

He had no trouble convincing them. They all agreed to the idea except for Amani, whom no one had seen. Ehab was excited, determined to photograph the surgery, and Nagy offered to let them use his apartment as the operating room. Both of them promised to help with whatever Tarek needed. Yehya agreed to the plan, too, but he wanted to wait a few days in case Alfat returned, to see if she would agree to assist. She hadn't been in her usual place for a few days. Tarek set a time with Nagy when the two of them could take a look at his apartment and prepare a room with the lighting and furniture he needed, and then he left them.

As soon as he returned to the hospital, he wrote the agreed-upon date and time on a scrap of paper, doodling around it in pencil so he wouldn't forget, and put it in a prominent place on his desk. His flipped through the pages of the file, as he'd become so used to doing, and with a yawn he noticed that his three visits to the queue had been recorded. Each one was marked with the date and time, but the space left for Alfat's answer was still blank. A few days later, Nagy told him that Alfat still hadn't returned, and that their worst suspicions had been confirmed: she had become the first person to disappear from the queue.

After her disappearance, they began to work faster: Tarek and Nagy brought the date forward, and Ehab went looking for a camera better than the one he could borrow from the newspaper. After he bought one, he didn't leave Yehya, who had begun to suffer from fainting spells and refused to leave his place. He'd given Nagy the task of searching the queue for Alfat, and told him to pay careful attention. Haunted by dark premonitions of losing Yehya, and Amani, too, Nagy busied himself with following the news provided by the woman with the short hair, and positioned himself near Um Mabrouk's stall and chairs, waiting for the appointed hour. Nothing new emerged while he was there. A tense atmosphere had settled over the queue, and more arguments arose. New rumors about the man standing on the roof of the Northern Building surfaced, too, but Nagy was focused only on finding Alfat.

Several days went by, and Tarek conducted trial runs in the hospital and finalized the list of equipment that he would need to take to Nagy's apartment. Sabah didn't understand why he was creeping around and disappearing off to secret activities, or why he was spending fewer hours reclining in his office alone. She tried to get it out of him, but he told her nothing. But the waiting overwhelmed him, and after a few days, Tarek lost his nerve. His commitment had flickered and waned, and he came up with a plausible excuse to delay his appointment with Nagy to prepare the apartment. Consumed by fear, he worried that he'd been too hasty with his idea and that this single act now could destroy his future forever. He read the file again; it contained no details of his visits to Yehya, or his proposal to conduct the operation at Nagy's house, but he knew he must be under surveillance. The moment that details of his first trip to the queue had appeared in the file, his name had moved from the space beside "Attending Physician" to the pages within. Now, it was now among those in Document No. 6 under the heading *Follow-Up*.

After two sleepless nights he made his decision, and resolved to gamble everything to fulfill his promise. He called Nagy to confirm the time, and then requested a whole week of vacation, something he'd never done during his whole time at the hospital. Sabah spread a web of rumors around him; she said he was going to marry another doctor from his clinic, and that he was preparing to travel abroad, and when he stopped signing in or out, without confirming or denying any of the rumors, she said that perhaps he'd followed in the steps of the head nurse, whose whereabouts still no one knew.

He returned home on foot after finishing his first task at Nagy's; the room was ready for them, and for the bullet. He got into bed, drew the sheets over him, and slept more deeply than he had for a long time. He dressed as soon as he awoke and headed straight to his office. He walked into the hospital without seeing anyone, pulled out the file, and opened it to the final page to read what had been written about the hours he'd spent at Nagy's. But there was no record of his visit at all, not a single line or the slightest indication that he'd been there. It was strange. This was the first time nothing new had been recorded about Yehya. He scoured the pages again, looking for his name, or anything that had been added, and then saw something that he hadn't initially noticed. On the bottom of the page there was a line he'd somehow missed: *Yehya Gad el-Rab Saeed spent one hundred and forty nights of his life in the queue.*

The previous page covered the day before yesterday, and then the updates stopped. Tarek sank into thought, confused, his chest tightening. Everything that had happened swirled in his mind as if it were one long, uninterrupted scene. He sat there in silence, calm, his gaze fixed on the opposite wall. There was no need to read the pages of the file another time. He automatically reached into his pocket, but he'd left his favorite pencil in the pocket of his coat, which was at home. He took a blue pen from his desk drawer instead, and as he hesitated for a moment on the paper it left a small dot of ink on the page. Then quickly, he added a sentence by hand to the bottom of the fifth document. He closed the file, left it on his desk, and rose.